CODY MEMORIAL LIBRARY
SOUTHWESTERN UNIVERSITY
GEORGETOWN, TEXAS 78626

W9-CML-560

WITHDRAWN

A. FRANK SMITH, JR. LIBRARY CENTER
Southwestern University Library
CF   C272M   Cassedy, Sylv
      M.E. and Morton /

3 3053 00122 1555

CF C272m

Cassedy, Sylvia.

DATE DUE

1 1994		
APR 07 1998		
DEC 01 2003		

GAYLORD No. 2333   PRINTED IN U.S.A.

208860

M. E. AND MORTON

ALSO BY SYLVIA CASSEDY

Behind the Attic Wall

M. E. AND MORTON

Sylvia Cassedy

Thomas Y. Crowell   New York

M. E. and Morton
Copyright © 1987 by Sylvia Cassedy
All rights reserved. No part of this book may be
used or reproduced in any manner whatsoever without
written permission except in the case of brief quotations
embodied in critical articles and reviews. Printed in
the United States of America. For information address
Thomas Y. Crowell Junior Books, 10 East 53rd Street,
New York, N.Y. 10022. Published simultaneously in
Canada by Fitzhenry & Whiteside Limited, Toronto.

Library of Congress Cataloging-in-Publication Data
Cassedy, Sylvia.
    M. E. and Morton.

    Summary: Eleven-year-old Mary Ella, ashamed that her
older brother Morton is a slow learner and longing for
a friend of her own, is astonished when the flamboyant
new girl on the block picks Morton for a friend.
    [1. Brothers and sisters—Fiction.   2. Learning
disabilities—Fiction.   3. Friendship—Fiction]
I. Title.   II. Title: ME and Morton.
PZ7.C268515Me 1987   [Fic]   85-48251
ISBN 0-690-04560-3
ISBN 0-690-04562-X (lib. bdg.)

Designed by Al Cetta
3 4 5 6 7 8 9 10

CF
C272m

For Ned

208860

M. E. AND MORTON

PROLOGUE

Once, back in third grade, my friend Wanda from school told me something so scary I never forgot it.

I was visiting in her beautiful bedroom on Calvin Boulevard, which is the street where all my rich school friends live, and after we had sat there for a while, not doing anything, I said, "Let's play poor children."

She stared at me. "Poor Children? I don't have it." She thought it was a board game or something.

"No," I said. "I mean, let's play we're poor. Let's play that all the stuff in this room is really junk. Let's play that we're sisters and we have no mother and father and we live here all by ourselves and we have to beg for money."

At first I had to do most of the pretending, because she didn't know how to play, but after a while she got really good at it, and the game lasted all afternoon. We played that her four-poster bed, with its pink ruffled canopy and frilly pillow, was a broken-down shack with no walls and a cardboard roof. We played that the vanity table, with its pale flowered skirt, was our school—a Gypsy tent with tattered sides and a dirt floor where we scratched out our lessons with a stick. Its cushioned bench was a mongrel at the door.

"Let's pretend that it's raining outside," I said, huddling on the bed, my hands over my head.

"No, *snowing*." She was really getting to like this a lot. "It's snowing all the way up to the roof, and we have nothing to wear except these old rags."

"And all we have to eat is some dry bread," I said.

"That we found in a garbage pail, and it has blue mold on it," she shouted.

"And we drink snow that we collect in cups."

"No, in our *bare hands*. We don't have any cups. In our bare hands that we can't move because our fingers are frozen solid."

"And for toys we have to play with trash in the street," I said. "We make dolls out of cigarette butts."

"With candy wrappers for dresses."

"And dead grass for hair." We were both shouting by now.

[4]

"And we take them skating on those little patches of ice where people spat on the sidewalk."

"Yeah, that's where they skate. On frozen spit."

It was a lovely game.

But then her mother came in and spoiled it all. "Don't play that," she said. "That's not a nice game. Play something happy."

But it *was* happy. "Why did she say that?" I asked Wanda when her mother had left. "Why can't we play poor children?" I asked, although I thought I knew: Her mother didn't want us to play poor children because she thought *I* was poor. She thought that because I lived over on Jefferson Place, and not on Calvin Boulevard, *my* house probably had a tin roof, too, and no walls, and that when it snowed I had to huddle in the middle of the floor. She thought because I went to school on a scholarship, I probably ate moldy bread like the poor sisters in the game, and drank melted snow from my hands. She thought I wore rags to school and skated little cigarette dolls on frozen spit. She thought it wasn't polite of Wanda to play a game that was the same as my real life.

I didn't think about the dead parents part.

"Why can't we play poor?" I asked, not wanting to know.

"Because if you play something bad it will come true," she said.

"What?" I couldn't believe what I had heard.

"Yeah. Make-believe games come true. The bad ones."

"They do?" I stared at her a long time. "If you play poor you *get* poor?" I began to imagine what it would be like if all of a sudden I had to wear rags and eat moldy bread and move away from Jefferson Place. Not that Jefferson Place is so great; it isn't, really, but my apartment building is pretty nice, with a green awning over the front door and everything, and, anyway, it's where I live. What if I had to move somewhere else, to some shack without walls where the snow blew in, and the rain, too? Someplace near a tattered school with a dirt floor and a mongrel growling at the door?

"I knew somebody once who played broken leg," Wanda went on, "and she *got* a broken leg. *Two* broken legs, as a matter of fact, because she played the game twice. She was in a wheelchair for a year."

"She was?" Wheelchair was one of my favorite games. I played it in my head all the time. I'd be terribly sick in my game—gravely ill, the doctor would say—and I'd spend all my days in a padded chair with great big wheels at its sides. Each morning my mother and father would wrap a blanket around my frail legs and take turns pushing me along the sunny paths in the park. People would look at me as we went by and then look away, not wanting to stare, but one or two would stop anyway and ask, "What happened?"

My mother's answer would float over my head. "She's gravely ill," she would say, and I would repeat the words to myself, liking them, especially the "gravely" part. Gravely. It reminded me of burials and mounds of earth. Then whoever it was would turn out to be a talent scout or someone like that, and he'd make me a poster girl for some disease with initials, and my picture would be in buses and subway cars all over the city. The *country*.

I also played scarlet fever and funeral—my own funeral, where everybody came and said how nice I had been and how smart.

"Make-believe games come true?" I asked again. "Even if you don't play them out loud? Even if you just play them to yourself, in your head?"

"Yeah, it doesn't matter. It's like someone is inside you all the time, listening, and they make it come true, like a bad wish."

"A bad wish?"

"Yeah, sort of."

"How soon?" I asked in a whisper. "How soon do they come true?"

"I don't know." She was smoothing out the bed now and replacing the pillow, which meant it was time for me to go home. "Sometimes it takes a while."

After that, I stopped playing wheelchair and funeral and poor children. I played games where only nice things happened.

I played rich.

I played twins.

I played movie star.

I played funnies. Each day I opened the newspaper to the funny pages and picked out a comic strip with a family I liked. Then I pretended to live with them—with Blondie and Dagwood, or with Charlie Brown. I followed them around their houses, walking my fingers from frame to frame, entering their rooms, belonging to them, whispering their names. "Hello, Blondie," I'd say. "It's me—Mary Ella." And she would answer, "Oh, Mary Ella. How nice you look today, with the red highlights in your hair and all."

I played Easter egg, which was a game I made up after my Aunt Sophia came for Easter dinner one day and gave me one of those frosted plaster eggs where you can see whole scenes of rabbit families when you hold them up to your eye.

I played First Lady.

About a year after I visited Wanda in her bedroom, I asked her how come she had played poor children with me if she had known that make-believe games came true, and she just looked at me. She didn't even remember having said that.

I remembered, though, because she was right: *half* right. Make-believe games do come true, but not the bad ones, with the bad wishes. It's the *good* make-believe games that come true.

I know, because one of mine did.

But not the way you'd think.

JUNE

CHAPTER ONE

The awning goes up in front of my apartment building every March, and it's the first green of spring to appear on Jefferson Place. It isn't even real green. It's the color you get when you forget to leave a space for the sun in your painting, and you have to yellow it in right over the blue sky. Gray-green, really, but it's a color I like; and each year, although I have seen it appear many times, it takes me by surprise. I turn the corner on my way home from school one day and there it is—a long shell of canvas stretching like a giant caterpillar from the doorway of my building to the curb.

All winter long, my street—with its vacant awning frame, its bare trees and hedges, its empty fire escapes, its blank sidewalks—looks like an unfilled page in a coloring book: all hollow spaces and dark lines. Now, though, suddenly, the first of those outlined spaces has been colored in. The awning frame, naked as a skeleton from September until March, is spread with lovely green, and I hold my books against my chest—hug them, really—as I contemplate it from the corner.

Later, little by little, more green comes to color the open spaces on Jefferson Place. Slender stripes of moss fill in, as though with a careful crayon, the narrow bands between the paving blocks, and black-green leaves, so brittle they snap in two when you fold them in half, sprout among the tangles of the hedge across the street. Soon, pots of spiky plants appear between the railings of the fire escapes, and three weeks or so after the awning goes up, the framework of branches on the maple at the corner is spread with a gray-green awning of its own. But it is that first stretch of green, that sudden bloom of canvas on the frame above my door, that lets me know for certain spring has come.

The awning itself doesn't really provide much protection from anything, as awnings should. It's full of holes, for one thing, so it's no use in the rain, and it offers no shelter from the snow either, because it isn't up when there *is* snow. But we always gather under it anyway, just as cats collect under a car, because it seems like a safe place to be.

Also, the awning tells the name of my house. "275 Coolidge Court 275," it says, in gray-white letters along its hem. All the apartment buildings on Jefferson Place have names, although none of the others has an awning, and all the names except one are those of presidents. Van Buren Arms. Monroe Court. Polk Terrace. (The only way I knew that Polk had been a president was that his name is woven into the doormat of the apartment house next door, and once, when my teacher asked who Henry Ward Beecher was, I raised my hand immediately and said he was a president, too. But Beecher Mansions, it turned out, is the one building on Jefferson Place that is named after somebody else.)

Another good thing about my awning has nothing to do with the green canvas part, but with the metal legs that support its frame at the curb: two upside-down V's, slender and strong and perfect for turning somersaults on. Every now and then someone will leave a game on the pavement, go over to those bars, and turn a somersault, quick as those toy bears that flip, feet over head, when you squeeze the two wooden rods at their sides.

I was turning a somersault myself, or trying to, the day Polly first appeared on Jefferson Place, and that is why, in my earliest memory of her, her face is upside down. It was the second week in June, and my school had already closed for the summer. No one else's had, though, so I was all alone on the block, and I was feeling good. I like it when everyone is in school and I have the street to myself. Also, I was wearing shorts outside for the first time all year—purple nylon shorts with those built-in underpants that are really designed for boys—and I liked the feel of elastic tight around my thighs and of the air moving up and down my legs. And the privet hedge across the street had just begun to bloom. Everywhere among the leaves were fuzzy flowers, pale as soda foam, that smell of beginning summer, of new shorts, of heat, of games in the street. I love that smell.

I was gripping the awning bars hard and leaning far, far back, practising my somersault, with the top of my head about to touch the ground, when I suddenly found myself gazing upside down into the face of a girl I had never seen before. The odd thing was that for a moment her face didn't look upside down at all. A pink Band-Aid taped across her forehead looked to me like a grim smile in the center of a broad chin, and her hair—a tangle of loops like those script ℓ's I scribble around the faces of my drawings—became, from that angle, a frizzy beard. She looked, in fact, like one of those trick pictures where you see either a bald man with lots of whiskers or a curly-haired child, depending on which way you hold them up.

The fact is, I really couldn't turn a somersault at all, although I practised a lot when no one was around. So, as soon as I realized I was being watched, I held still and pretended instead to be examining some exciting event on the underside of the awning, like a circus acrobat or something. Anyway, I gazed carefully upward for a long time, hanging on to the awning bars and scraping the ends of my hair against the sidewalk. I especially wanted this new girl, whoever she might be, to notice my long hair, which somebody once said had red highlights and which somebody else once said was my one nice feature.

I wanted her to notice a lot of things about me. The way I laced my sneakers, for instance, so that the bow was at the bottom of the row of holes instead of at the top, and the way my necklace shone like real gold. I had been tieing my sneakers upside down for four months, hoping somebody would notice them, but nobody ever did, and nobody ever noticed my necklace either, with its one hundred and fifty-four S's linked, tail to tail, into a chain so fine I could coil it into the letters of my name.

Every night, when I was alone in my room, I would pretend that someone was watching me from my window and admiring all those nice things about me. That was how I played Easter egg, the game I began when Aunt Sophia gave me that egg with the scene inside. In my game, *I* lived in one of those eggs and some strange girl peered at me through the glass. "Oh, hey," she'd say, "look how she ties her sneakers!" Or, "Look at that necklace with all those golden S's." Just the day before, I had sewn my initials in little red cross-stitches on all my T-shirts, and the girl at my egg window had noticed them and said nice things.

Now I wanted this new girl to notice them, too, and to wonder about them. "How come it says 'ME' on her T-shirt?" I wanted her to say to herself. I wanted her to wonder, too, why I was out on the street at a time when everyone else was in school, and to guess finally that I was home not because I was sick or cutting classes, but because I went to a private school that closed for the summer earlier than everybody else's.

Most of all, I wanted her to notice that I lived in Coolidge Court, the only building on the block with its own awning, the only one with furniture in the lobby and metal blinds on all the windows instead of paper shades. The best house on the block. Mine. I wanted her to notice that, and to wish that she were me.

It was nice hanging there, letting my hair fall to the ground, feeling the eyes of this new girl linger on my red highlights, on the chain at my neck, on my embroidered letters, on my sneaker laces, on *me*—the one who went to private school and lived in the only building on the block with an awning.

I hung there so long that when I finally straightened out, I felt dizzy. The privet hedge across the way drifted out of focus, and a storm of silver fireflies took flight before my eyes. It was a while before I could turn to meet her eyes, but when at last I did, I found that the sidewalk was empty, and the new girl who was to have been my audience had, in fact, moved on and wasn't there at all.

CHAPTER TWO

I didn't see her again until the following week. I was under the awning that time, too, but not practising somersaults. Instead, I was sitting on the curb, making sunrays with a Popsicle stick out of a puddle in the street. Doing nothing, really. Everyone was still in school and the afternoon was quiet. Suddenly, though, there came a clicking sound, and I looked up to see her, the new girl, on the opposite sidewalk, running a piece of chalk against the iron pickets that surrounded the privet. She walked quickly, leaving behind her, like a message spurted out by a skywriting plane, an even row of soft, pale dashes.

A Band-Aid was still spread like a grin across her forehead, but the tangled loops of her hair were bundled now behind her head with a piece of string—the kind you tie up packages with—and this time she was wearing lipstick. *Purple* lipstick that went outside the lines at the corners of her mouth. I watched her secretly, with my chin on my knees, as she progressed along the street.

When she reached the end of the iron pickets, she paused in front of the privet and searched for something among its leaves. For what? I wondered. For anything, it could have been; things always get caught in the tangles of that hedge—nice things, some of them: jack balls, for instance, that have escaped from some wild throw, and squares of colored cellophane that turn the sky to fire when you hold them to your eye. Feathers, too—gray, usually, but sometimes blue—to smooth between your fingertips; and money, even—Henry found a dollar bill there once, folded neatly like a soft green moth among the twigs.

She could have been looking for any of these things, but, as it happened, what she wanted was a leaf. She plucked one off carefully, and I waited for her to do with it what I always do with privet leaves—fold it in half and listen to it snap. Instead, she curled it up and put it in her mouth.

Hey, I wanted to call out, *don't eat that! It'll make you sick!* I knew, because I had once tried eating a privet leaf myself, choosing one that was crisp and shiny as vinyl and curling it over, just as she had done, before sinking my teeth into it. It hadn't really made me sick, but it had been bitter, and I had spat on the sidewalk a long time afterward, trying to rinse the taste from my tongue. *Don't!* I wanted to cry, but by then she had picked off another and was eating that one, too. Anyway, I wouldn't have called out to her at all. I didn't even want her to know I was watching.

I looked at her secretly, though, for a long time. First I watched her eat the leaves, and then I inspected her clothes. They were not like what anybody else I knew ever wore. Her skirt, for one thing, came far below her knees, and it seemed to be about fifty years old. It was made of wide bands of black, yellow, and red, and it looked like those costumes we wear year after year in school plays—those of us who don't get good parts and end up being peasants. She wore it with a plaid flannel shirt that was too big on her and, any-way, was too warm for a day in June. Together they made her look like—what? An outsider, sort of, like someone from someplace far away, and I wondered suddenly why *she* wasn't in school in the middle of June.

Maybe she was foreign, I thought. Maybe she had just come from someplace where everybody wore long skirts and ate privet leaves. Maybe she needed someone who could teach her things and show her around. A guide. Maybe *I* could be her guide. I could teach her new words in English. "This is a gold chain," I could tell her, hooking my thumb under my necklace and

Pretty soon the public-school kids would come home, and one of them—Deirdre, most likely—would spot the new girl and know immediately what to say, and the new girl, even if she knew no English, would smile, and they would go off together. After a while, they would come up to me, hand in hand, and Deirdre would say, "This is Gemma. I'm teaching her English. Say 'awning,' Gemma." That's the way things always end up with me.

The pink end of the Popsicle stick had turned black in the water, and the other end, pale as cream a few moments ago, was becoming gray in my hand. The new girl began to rub her chalk against the sidewalk, drawing something, and once she looked up at me, but I didn't return her glance. She probably wasn't foreign at all, I decided. Lots of people wore clothes that didn't match, and lots of people ate crazy things—pencil erasers, for instance, and paper reinforcements, and those dried bits of skin that grow around your thumb. Privet leaves were no crazier to eat than thumbnail skin, when you stopped to think about it. And she probably wasn't a runaway, either. Nobody would run away *to* Jefferson Place. Still, it would be nice to have a new friend, especially before anybody else had a chance to get to her.

Soon, I told myself, my sun puddle would dry up, and when it did I would walk across the street and say something. What? *Do you like privet leaves? Do you want this Popsicle stick? Is your name Gemma?* What could I say? *What's that you're drawing?* That might be good. *Can I see your picture?* Something like that. I would rehearse it first so it came out just right. Then, by the time Deirdre and everybody else arrived, the new girl would belong to me. We would sit side by side under the privet, playing hangman on the sidewalk with her chalk, and after a while we would walk under the green awning together, and go into my lobby with all the nice furniture and up to my apartment with the metal blinds on the windows, and she would be my friend. "Let's see your picture," I practised into the puddle.

But the puddle didn't dry up at all, and we sat there a long time, I with the oily sun at my feet, she with the chalk drawing at hers. Every so often a car would pass between us and cut off my view of her, the way a head in front of a movie projector suddenly darkens the screen, but the rest of the time I could sneak looks at her whenever I wanted. Now and then she would look at me and then return to her chalk, making quick, long strokes on the sidewalk, shading them in with the side of her fist, tilting her head to inspect what she had drawn. Soon she began looking at me more often, casting her eyes up and then down, up and down, while the chalk moved back and forth, faster and faster, and I realized all at once that what she was drawing was a picture of me.

I kept my eyes down after that, and held very still, with my sneakers lined up and my head just right so she could copy my highlights and my gold chain and the M. E. on my T-shirt. Nobody had ever drawn my portrait before, and it felt nice, being examined that way, being reproduced, having a whole other *me* created across the street, right next to the girl I wanted to have as a friend.

I turned my lips up a little so that she would give my sidewalk face a smile, and then, after a while, I said hello, silently, thinking somehow that she could copy that, too, and make it speak from my chalk mouth. *Hello*, I said in my head, *I'm Mary Ella*. And I imagined the words rising out of the white powder to the girl across the street. *I've just finished sixth grade, but I'm a year younger than everybody else in my class because I skipped fourth grade. I go to the Agnes Daly School, which is this special private school for smart kids. I'm exceptionally smart, but I'm also quite nice, nicer than anyone else on Jefferson Place, and I've been told that I'm unusually sensitive for my age. That's what grown-ups always say about me. I won first prize in an essay contest once, and Mrs. Pierce . . .*

"Who's that?" Suddenly the girl across the street spoke, and I looked up, startled, thinking that she had actually heard the words I was trying to send over to my mouth on the pavement. But she wasn't looking at the picture at all, and she wasn't looking at me, either—the real me, that is. Her eyes were on the corner, and I saw now that all the public-school kids were coming home from school. *"Who's that?"* she asked again, and I knew at once that she had spotted Morton on his way up the street.

Morton is the dumbest kid on the block, and he is also the ugliest. Last year he was only one grade ahead of me, but he's three years older, and every summer he has to go to summer school to catch up with everybody else, but he never does. He always wears a dumb gray T-shirt with a peeling Mickey Mouse or Snoopy on it, and his socks are always sliding into his shoes so that his heels show. Actually, he isn't that ugly— his hair is a rather nice shade of red, and his eyes are large and dark. On anyone else, in fact, his face wouldn't look at all bad; on him, though, it looks ugly. His head hangs down on his chest all the time, and he shuffles his feet as though he's trying to pick up static on a carpet. Also, in winter, his hat comes down to his nose so that he looks like a fire hydrant, and sometimes when he loses his gloves he wears ugly gray socks on his hands, which he waves around like paws.

The other thing about Morton is that he is my brother.

CHAPTER THREE

"Who *is* that?" the girl asked again, but I returned my eyes to the wet sun with its crooked rays and twisted rainbows, and pretended not to hear.

"Hey," she said, louder this time. "Who's that kid?"

"Who?" I answered, not looking up. That, after all, turned out to be the first word I spoke to the new girl across the street—"Who?"—and I said it into my knees.

"With the red T-shirt."

"Who?" I looked up quickly. "Oh, him. That's Charles." I finally looked into her face, giving her my friendly smile, the one that makes my eyes pinch together and my cheeks stick out.

"Cute," she said. "Who's the one in the back?" Morton always walks in the back, partly because his walk is so slow, but mostly because nobody wants to walk with him.

The wet rays were shrinking into the puddle now,

first one and then another, and I tried to stretch them out again with the end of the Popsicle stick.

"I said, who's the one in the back?"

I looked toward the corner again, squinting into the light and pretending, as I do when I misread a word on the blackboard in school, to be nearsighted. "Which?" I asked. As if there was more than one.

"In the Mickey Mouse shirt," she answered. "With the walk."

"Oh, that," I said, looking at my feet again. "Morton."

"What?"

"Morton," I said, louder this time, but not really loud.

"Morton? That's that kid's name? *Morton?* Who would give anybody a name like that?"

"I don't know," I said. "There's an Ezra on this block, too."

"So?"

I didn't say anything. I had always thought Ezra was a dumber name than Morton, but Morton was pretty bad, too. Morton.

Morton without the t. I had made that up once, a long time ago, but I had never told it to anyone, even though I thought it was pretty funny. Morton without the *t* spelled moron, and I couldn't understand why

[*31*]

208860 CODY MEMORIAL LIBRARY
SOUTHWESTERN UNIVERSITY
GEORGETOWN, TEXAS 78626

no one else had ever thought of it. Someday, probably, somebody would. Franklin, most likely. He was always thinking up things like that. Someday, he would shout down the street, "Hey, you know what? Take the *t* out of Morton and what do you get?" Then as soon as everybody else caught on, they would all start to laugh, and Franklin would get credit for something I had really thought up first. Still, I kept it to myself, because I knew everyone would immediately start calling Morton "Morton without the *t*," and I didn't especially want that, even though I had made it up.

"Dumb name," the girl across the street said.

In a little while, everyone would reach the awning, and in a little while after *that*, the new girl would belong to someone else—Deirdre, probably, or Justine. Maybe both.

"That's about the dumbest name I ever heard," she added, and in another minute she'd say something like "He's about the dumbest kid I ever saw."

"It's not really a first name," I said quickly. "It's his mother's maiden name."

There was a long silence. Then, "How come you know so much about him? How come you know all that, about his mother's maiden name and everything? Is he your boyfriend, or what?"

I stared at her. Did I look like someone who would pick Morton for a boyfriend?

"Is he?" she persisted.

"Is he what?"

"Your boyfriend."

I slipped the gold chain across my chin, letting its clasp dig into the back of my neck as I moved my head. "No," I answered.

"How come?"

"I have another boyfriend," I lied.

"Who? Ezra?"

"No. Someone who doesn't live around here. He goes to my school. I go to a private—"

"If he's not your boyfriend, how come you know all that stuff about him?"

I thrust my chin up quickly, and all at once the gold chain broke, spilling like a sudden stream of water into my hand.

"I bet he's your boyfriend," she said.

Everyone had reached the awning now, even Morton, but I didn't turn around to say hello. I felt them move about behind me and bump into each other like a bustle of pigeons, and I listened to the footsteps of those who continued up the street, but I looked only at the gold pool in my palm, stirring it with a finger.

"Hey, Morton," the girl across the street suddenly called out.

Don't answer, I said to myself, closing my eyes tight. *Don't answer, don't answer, don't answer.*

"What?" he answered.

"Come here. I want to ask you something," and I heard him shuffle across the street.

"Hey, Morton," she said. "Is that your girlfriend?"

"What?" he said. He always says "what," and once my mother took him to an ear doctor because she thought maybe he was deaf. "Hard of hearing" is what she called it, but there was nothing the matter with his ears. He says "what" to give himself time to think up something else to say, only the ear doctor didn't tell her that. He said my brother was faking. I think my mother was disappointed that Morton wasn't deaf. Hard of hearing is better than dumb.

Anyway, the girl across the street didn't get a chance to repeat her question, because just then someone behind me called out to her. "Hey," she cried. "You new here?" It wasn't Deirdre *or* Justine. It was Ina, and the next moment I opened my eyes to see all the girls on my block walking across the street toward the girl who was going to wait in the shed for my packages of grapes and mittens, who was going to repeat "awning" and "gold chain" after me, who was going to play hangman with me under the privet, who was going to be my friend.

CHAPTER FOUR

Pretty soon they were all telling their names—the new girl said hers was Polly—and their ages and what grades they were in and where they lived and which ones were sisters. They were all talking at once, and I couldn't tell who was saying what, but all of a sudden there was a pause and someone noticed the picture on the sidewalk. "Hey," she said. "Did you make that? That's a really good picture. Is it supposed to be you?"

"Me? No."

"Then how come it says 'ME' on it?"

"It's a picture of her, over there." Polly pointed with her chin. "With the writing on her shirt."

Everybody suddenly turned to look at me. "You mean Mary Ella?" "That's supposed to be her?" "Hey, Mary Ella, come and see what you look like." "Hey, it looks just like you, with the stringy hair and all, and those crooked letters on your T-shirt."

I half rose, wanting to join them, not wanting to,

wanting to again. But finally I sat down, knowing it was too late. They all belonged to each other now, and I somehow belonged with Morton, who remained, as I did, apart from the group. All the other boys had already gone home, and the rest of the street was quiet. It would have been a good time for Morton to get away, but he just stood there, as I knew he would, waiting for the new girl, for Polly, to notice him again and to ask her question: "Hey, Morton, is that your girlfriend?"

Morton never runs away from anything, no matter how dangerous, not because he's brave, but because he's dumb. Once, long ago, Franklin found an old baby carriage in his lobby, and he offered to give everybody a ride in it. All morning long he ran up and down the block with it, wheeling two, sometimes three kids at a time in its canvas sling and singing "Rockabye Baby" at the top of his lungs. Morton and somebody else were having their rides when the man who owned the carriage came after us, and everyone except Morton ran away. Morton just sat there, waiting, looking like a circus clown in a baby suit, until the man tipped him out onto the ground. I watched from behind a car, scared, as Morton was marched up the street by the collar, his head bouncing back and forth like a punched balloon, and I wonder even now what happened when the man finally led him into the shed down the block.

The girls across the street were still admiring the drawing on the sidewalk, putting their heads to one side and the other as they examined first the picture and then me. "You know what?" Justine said, taking Polly's piece of chalk. "You left something out," and she crouched over the pavement. "You forgot to put in her book bag." She began making big chalk strokes on the ground. "The Agnes Daly School book bag." "Daaaaay-ly," she pronounced it, letting her voice linger long and high on the first syllable.

"And put in the hat," Ina added. "Put in the Agnes Daly School hat with the worms."

They're not worms; they're laurel leaves, and they curl around the initials of my school on a little gold emblem that decorates my hat and the pocket of my blazer. It's the part of my school uniform that I like best, and I draw pictures of it all over the binding of my loose-leaf notebook, and sometimes in the dust on the hood of a parked car. They're *leaves*, I wanted to say, not *worms*. But I didn't.

Morton had edged closer to the group and was by now leaning over to look at the picture with everybody else, so that suddenly I was the only one who didn't belong. "It looks just like you," he said, repeating what

somebody had already said, "with the hat and all."
That's the way he talks lots of times—he says other
people's words as though he'd thought of them himself.

There was a long silence, and then I heard, "Hey!"
The voice was loud and sharp, and it took me by
surprise, even though it was my own. "Hey, Morton!"
I heard myself call, the voice seeming to float down
from a rooftop. "Hey, Morton, you know what?" I was
standing up now, one foot on the curb, one off, as
though I were about to run a race. "Hey, Morton!" I
yelled. "Take the *t* out of your name and guess what's
left!" And then, "Hey, Morton without the *t*!" and
all their faces blurred like paints in a dish of water as
they turned slowly to look at me.

Later, after everyone had gone home, I bent over
to examine the chalk picture on the sidewalk. Parts
of it had already been erased by being walked on, so
that one elbow was missing and the M. E. was smudged,
but the rest of it was still there. It looked just like all
those pictures of girls everybody draws—a fat U for a
face, a square hat, broom-straw hair, round eyes with
lashes like sunrays, and mittens instead of hands. No
highlights in the hair. No upside-down sneaker laces.
No laces at all, for that matter, and no sneakers either.
Each leg ended in a sharp point. And no gold necklace.

I stared at the picture a long time and then, un-coiling the broken chain from my palm, I carefully curved it across the chalk throat on the sidewalk. It looked nice there, glowing in the sun like real gold, and I felt good, as though I had given a present to someone poor. It's for you, I said into the eyes with their sunray lashes, and with the tip of my finger I stretched the chalk lips into a small smile.

Ina had been the first one in the group to catch on to my joke about Morton's name. Polly had been the last. "That's pretty good," Ina had said, looking over at me as I stood on the curb, and I smiled at her. "Morton without the *t*," she cried out to the others. "Get it? Morton without the *t*." She clapped her hands in time to the words.

Everyone else stood around, not understanding at first, looking at Ina, looking at me, and then finally catching on, but still not joining in. Not right away. Not until someone said, "But Mary Ella said it *first*. She made it *up*," and then they all took up the cry, flapping around Morton like a ring of hungry sea gulls.

Polly watched them from the iron fence along the privet, and I watched from the curb across the street. "Morton without the *t*!" they sang, over and over, until it became a chant—"Morton with*out* the *t*! Morton with*out* the *t*!"—and they locked hands, fencing Morton in. Suddenly Polly's mouth twitched a little and her eyebrows rose, and I knew that she, too, had finally caught on. At that moment I crossed the street and the circle opened up to let me in.

We all sang together after that—all of us except Polly, who stood at the privet and watched—and we sang as loud as we could, keeping time with our feet and pumping our arms up and down.

I sang the loudest of all. And although I didn't look at Polly, I felt her eyes on my back, and I liked knowing that she was watching me, that she was watching all of us—Ina and Deirdre and Justine and everybody— while we sang the song that I'd made up.

Morton never caught on to the joke at all. Instead, he looked around with that dumb expression he has, and tried to join in, which is another thing he does all the time. He joins in anything that's going on, even when it's directed against him, because he doesn't even know he's being kept out. "Morton without the tea," he called out, trying to break into the circle. "Morton without the coffee," and when everybody laughed, he laughed too, and said it again. Four times.

I rubbed out the face first, smudging the chalk with my sneaker sole until the lips with their twin peaks spread into a pale egg and the eyelashes faded to pow-der. Then I worked on the hat, the tattered ME, the book bag, and the pointy legs, until there was nothing left on the sidewalk but a gray smear, shapeless as a scrap of cloud, and the gold chain, tan now in the dusk.

CHAPTER FIVE

When Aunt Sophia gave me the Easter egg that day
long ago, she lifted it up to my eye and whispered,
"Look inside, Mary Ella. There's a surprise in there,"
and she smiled at me in that way she had. "It's magic,"
she told me as I peered through its dark round window,
and she was right. It *was* magic, and I caught my breath
at the vision of a whole rabbit household in a sunlit
room—with a mother rabbit, a father rabbit, and a
child rabbit, all dressed in little clothes and seated
around a table set with bowls of wooden eggs.

Off to one side was a fireplace with a paper flame
in its hearth, and along the rounded walls were tiny
pictures: of flowers, of birds, of other rabbits—a grandfather and a grandmother. At the far end was a little
rabbit bed, big enough for the child rabbit, and across
it lay a pale-blue spread.

I stood there a long time, gazing at it all and saying,
"Oh, Aunt Sophia, look. Look at the table and the

chairs and the pictures. Look at the bed. And the little eggs!" Look at this, look at that. "Look how tiny!" I wanted to break the glass with my finger and hop the little bodies about from chair to fireplace to bed. I wanted to roll the tiny eggs against my thumb and to fan the flame in the hearth until it leaped up.

"And the clothes, Mary Ella," Aunt Sophia said, so close to me I could feel her breath against my ear. "Look at the clothes. Look carefully at the father rabbit's jacket. Do you see what's on the left-hand side just below the collar? It's a *pocket*, and there's something very wonderful inside."

"There is?"

"Yes. It's a little gold coin. A rabbit coin, with a picture of the first rabbit president on one side, and the words BUNNY MONEY on the other. You can't see it, of course, but it's there all the same."

"How do you know?" I demanded. I didn't really care how she knew; I just wanted her to go on talking about the rabbits.

"Well, it *has* to be there, because that's the only pocket he has."

I held the egg in front of me and tapped at the little window, urging the rabbits to turn their heads, to look at me, to smile, to invite me in, to show me the coin—and that was how I began my game.

That night I pretended that my room was an Easter

egg, exactly like the one Aunt Sophia had given me, with a little bed and pictures on the walls and a fireplace and bowls of tiny eggs on the table. The Easter egg was held between the fingers of some giant girl whose eye filled my window, and I was the child rabbit she saw inside. "Oh, look!" she would cry, and she would watch me move about among my things, from table to fireplace to wall. "Look how tiny! Look at the little pictures and the eggs." Look at this, look at that. "Look at how beautiful the child rabbit is. Look at the highlights in her hair and her white dress."

Then she would start tapping at my window glass and calling to me. "Hey, Bunny," she would say. "Look at me," but I never would. I'd pretend not to know she was there, and I would struggle to keep from smiling while I felt her eye at the window, her lashes brushing against the pane.

I would feel her wishing things, too. She would wish she could reach through the window and move me about from place to place, to grasp me by the waist and bend my legs so that I would sit in my chair, or to straighten them out so I could be put on the little bed. She would wish she could cover my little rabbit body with a blanket and close my eyelids one at a time with her finger, saying, "Go to bed now, Bunny." But the window would be too small for her hand, and so she would just look in, filling the pane from top to sill with her dark, giant eye.

I would pretend that a father and a mother rabbit were in the egg room with me, and we would all sit together at the little table. "Happy Easter," I'd say to them every night, because it was always Easter Sunday inside the egg, and they would say "Happy Easter" back. "How pretty you look today," the mother rabbit would say, and I would smile, liking to hear that. Then we'd nibble at the little wooden eggs in our bowls, and later we'd take a walk around the room, just the three of us, with no brother rabbit or sister rabbit. First we'd stop at the pictures on the walls and say something nice about them: "Wow, look how blue that flower is," or "Hmm. Grandfather was some handsome rabbit," and we'd stop to warm our hands—our paws, whatever they were—at the fireplace.

Then I'd give the mother rabbit an Easter present— something nice, a flower maybe—and she'd say, "Oh, Mary Ella, this is the most beautiful flower I have ever seen. Look!" She'd hold it up for the father rabbit to see. "Oh, wow," he'd say, and he'd fasten it to the mother rabbit's hat. We'd all hold hands after that, liking the flower, liking each other.

Pretty soon the father rabbit would take out his paint set, and we'd all sit around the table and decorate the little wooden eggs in our bowls. We wouldn't speak. We'd just sit there, side by side, while dazzling little pictures took shape at the ends of our tiny brushes. Each night I'd paint a bowl of daisies on an egg. The bowl was a lovely blue and perfectly round, like a bubble, and the daisy petals looked cool and stiff, like real ones. "Exquisite," the mother rabbit would say, admiring it and shaking her head back and forth in disbelief. "Absolutely exquisite." She pronounced it the way Mrs. Pierce does in school: "EXquisite," she says. "Say it after me, boys and girls: EXquisite," and we do.

Finally, just before saying good night to me, the father rabbit would bend over and say, "Now I have something very special to show you," and that would be the best part of the game. With his paw he would reach into the little pocket on the left-hand side of his jacket and pull out the tiny gold coin. "Look!" he'd say, and he'd hold it up. Aunt Sophia was right: The head of a rabbit was on one side and the words BUNNY MONEY were on the other. But I knew something she didn't know: On the picture side was a little circle, so tiny you had to squint to see it, and inside were the initials M. E. The rabbit on the coin was *me*.

"Well," the father rabbit would say to me. "To-morrow we will go out and spend it. What shall we buy?" And I would always answer, "Oh, Father Rabbit, don't spend it at all. Just keep it in your pocket so we can have it for always," and that is what he would do. He'd slide it back into his pocket and then kiss me good night, while the eye of the giant girl watched between the slats of the blinds at the window.

CHAPTER SIX

When my *real* family sits at the table, there are four of us, not three, and when we go for a walk, as we do every Sunday afternoon, I have to walk ahead with Morton, because the paths in the park are too narrow for four. My father never offers to buy me something with money from his pocket, and my mother never tells me I'm pretty, although I try to get her to. "Oh, Mom," I said to her once as she braided my hair in front of the mirror. "Look how ugly I am. Who will ever want to marry me?" and I waited for her to say, "Oh, Mary Ella, you're not ugly at all. You're beautiful," but all she answered was, "Plenty of ugly women get married," and she tightened the braid at my neck so that my skin pulled and I cried out.

Also, we never paint pictures on eggs. On *anything*. My mother doesn't like to paint, my father has no time, and all Morton knows how to draw is those dumb houses where the chimney juts out from a triangle roof and the windows and the door make a face.

I like to paint, though, and my pictures in school are so good, some of them, that they hang in the art room for weeks, but I don't ever paint when I'm at home. I don't want my pictures hung up on the refrigerator door with Morton's dumb triangle roofs. When I bring home a picture from school I roll it up in a drawer, where its ends crinkle like chapped lips and the paper gets less and less white.

And, when I give my real mother a present, she doesn't say, "Oh, how beautiful!" like the mother rabbit in the egg. All she ever says is "Very nice," even though she knows my present is quite wonderful. "Very nice," she says, because what I give her is a whole lot better than what Morton gives her, and she has to pretend to like them both the same.

In fact, she doesn't like to get presents at all. Once, when Morton asked, "What do you want for Mother's Day?" all she could think of to say was "Obedience." Obedience! For *Mother's* Day.

She complains a whole lot about how disobedient Morton is, but she doesn't mean disobedient, really; she means dumb. He isn't disobedient at all. He doesn't sneak off to the movies when he's supposed to be studying, the way Ina's brother does, and he doesn't smoke cigarettes on the roof, like Ezra. He isn't smart enough to do things like that. Instead, he puts his clothes on crooked and he forgets to wipe his nose. I think she talks all the time about how disobedient he is because that's what she wishes he really were—disobedient instead of dumb.

As it happened, Morton already had a present for her that Mother's Day, but he asked her what she wanted anyway, hoping she would say "bookends," which is what he was planning to give her—wooden bookends that he had made in school and that were shaped like cats. He had carved them out with a jigsaw, tracing around the patterns his shop teacher had pasted down on two slabs of wood, but the saw blade had slipped, and the cats didn't match. They didn't even look like cats; they looked like dinosaurs, and his teacher had given him a D on them, because everything was crooked and the nails showed through, but Morton wrapped them up for a Mother's Day present, anyway. "What do you want for your present?" he asked her that day, and he laughed his dumb laugh because he had a secret and he was excited about it. When she said "Obedience," he just looked at her.

"Why don't you *buy* her a present?" I asked him then, because I didn't want her to see the terrible bookends, and also I didn't want her to have to say that my present was very nice. I had picked out a necklace for her that year—a string of tiny seashells, so thin you could see your fingers through them when you held them up to the sky, and so brittle they let out a tiny chime when their edges brushed. "You could get her an African violet from the five-and-ten," I told him. "They come in all kinds of colors—purple and pink and everything. You could get her any color you liked."

"I don't have any money," he answered, which was true. My mother had stopped giving him an allowance when she discovered that he had been giving it all away to Ezra. So she got bookends from Morton that year instead of an African violet, instead of obedience, and she put them next to my necklace and said they were both very nice. "Very nice," she said as she stood Morton's wooden cats side by side on the table, and "Very nice" when she held up my beautiful row of shells. *Very nice!* Even though the necklace hung from her fingers like a flurry of blossoms and tinkled with the softness of a mouse paw on glass.

Next Mother's Day, Morton didn't remember to buy her anything at all. He had forgotten the date, and I purposely hadn't reminded him. In secret, I went out to buy her a present of my own—a little glass prism that spilled rainbows all over the room when it caught the light—and in secret I gave it to her early that Sunday morning.

[*51*]

"Oh, Mary Ella!" she said, and she swung the prism around by its string, making the rainbows race around the walls. I think she really liked it, although she didn't say.

When Morton saw it, though, he finally remembered the day, and he went through the house looking for something to give her. What he found was a library book—a *library* book!—that my father had borrowed for himself and that had been lying on the coffee table for about a month. Morton wrapped it up in my tissue paper, and he made her a card, copying out the verse from the one I had bought and coloring a border around it with red crayon. Then he wrote "To Mother From Morton" on it and stuck it under a fold of the wrapping. He spelled Mother wrong, though—"To Moter," he wrote—and he spelled From wrong, too: Form.

My mother said his present was very nice, and she even kept it a week after it was due, pretending to read it now and then, but in the end she had to take it back, and at the same time she stopped admiring my prism.

It still hangs at the kitchen window, splattering tiny rainbows each morning on everything in the room: the refrigerator, the cereal bowls, the bread, the sink— even, at times, our faces, tinting our skin with thin, watery colors: reds and greens and blues, pale as a bruise. But my mother doesn't notice it at all.

CHAPTER SEVEN

When I finally went upstairs that evening, after singing my moron song to Morton, everybody was already in the kitchen. My father and brother were sitting at the table, and my mother was at the stove, making circles in a pot with a wooden spoon. "There's a new girl on the block," I told her before she could ask why I was late. "Her name is Polly," I said, going over to the sink and splashing water loudly on my hands. "She's my friend now," I shouted over the noise.

I don't have many friends. Before this summer, I really didn't have any—not the kind, anyway, who call you up on the phone a lot and borrow your clothes. Once someone asked me, "Which would you rather have, one really good friend or lots of half-good friends?" I said I didn't know, but what I wanted was both: one really good friend to have fun with, and a whole bunch of half-good friends to make me look popular. Mostly, all I have is one half-good friend and then some people

I play with now and then: Ina, maybe, or Deirdre, but they are best friends with each other, not with me. Until this summer, I never had a best friend. I am the only girl in my class who doesn't have one in school, and when we have to pick partners in gym, I always end up with the teacher.

But I pretend to my mother that I have lots of friends, so I won't be like Morton, who has none. I tell her a lot about Wanda and Iris from school, and Rhoda and Linnet. Actually, Wanda is my friend from the class I used to be in before I skipped, and there isn't any Linnet at all. I just like the name. "Why don't you invite them over?" my mother always asks, and I say they live too far away. They don't, really. They live on Calvin Boulevard, and sometimes I visit them, but I don't want them to see where I live. I don't want them to know that we eat dinner in the kitchen and hang our wash from a ceiling rack over the bathtub. I don't want them to see Morton. And besides, they wouldn't come anyway.

"You're late," my father said, looking up at me from the table.

"I was with my new friend, Pop," I answered.

Pop. I began calling my father Pop a long time ago, because that's what Wanda calls *her* father, and I thought maybe he would get to be like Wanda's father if he had the same name. Pop: someone who knows how to play Old Maid and who asks knock-knock jokes and reads the funnies. I feel silly calling him Pop now, though. Father would be better, or Wilson, which is his first name, although everybody calls him Bill. Or even Mr. Briggs. "Hi, Mr. Briggs," I could say, as though he were a visitor.

Most of the time I call him nothing at all, which is what he calls me. Last year, I asked him to call me M. E. "All my friends are going to call me that now," I said, "so maybe you should call me that, too," but all he said was "Mmm." He doesn't call me anything because he doesn't talk to me very much. He calls Morton by his name more than he calls me by mine, but that's because "Morton" is *all* he says to him. "Morton!" he says at the dinner table, and that means use a handkerchief or close your mouth when you chew.

Once, a long time ago, I wondered if he remembered my name at all, or my birthday, or how old I was, or what grade I was in, and I even tested him. I wrote out a questionnaire and pretended it was a form he had to fill out. "My teacher wants you to answer these questions," I told him. "It's so I can get promoted," and I handed him a paper with lots of headings and blank spaces: NAME . . . SEX . . . BIRTHDAY . . . NAME OF SCHOOL . . . GRADE IN SCHOOL . . . NAME OF TEACHER . . . AWARDS. . . .

Things like that, but he didn't fill it out at all. "Silly girl," he said, handing it back after glancing at it. Silly girl, and so I filled in the word "girl" for him next to where it said SEX, and I signed his name at the bottom: Wilson F. Briggs.

"What are used oars?" Morton suddenly asked, bending over the newspaper at the kitchen table. He was doing the crossword puzzle. He does it every night, although he doesn't really *do* it. He just puts in S's where there are plurals, and then he asks us to tell him all the rest of the answers. If there are still some empty squares after that, he fills them in with any letters at all. Mostly M's, for Morton. "It's a house," he says about the puzzle, "with a whole lot of rooms, and the letters live there."

He's fourteen years old and he still does that.

"That's stupid," I tell him. "That's not what you're supposed to do with a crossword puzzle. You're supposed to put in the right words so they fit together when they cross. That's why it's called *crossword.* Get it?" But he doesn't. "CROSS WORD!" I shout, and he looks at me with his dumb look and says "*tss,*" which is a sort of laugh he makes when people get mad at him. He never cries.

Except for once.

"What are used oars?" he asked my mother. She was still stirring the pot and the steam rose into her face, making a curtain on her glasses. On her ears, too, maybe, because she didn't answer.

"Used oars," he repeated, and when she still didn't answer, he said, "Five letters."

"I don't know, Morton," she finally said. "Put it away. We're about to eat."

"What do you *think* it is?" he insisted. "Used oars."

"I don't *know*, Morton. There's no word for that."

"It says it here," he said. "Five letters."

"You're reading it wrong," I said, turning to him from the sink. Water slid down my elbows and onto my stomach. "It's probably used *cars*," and I looked over to my mother so she would agree. So she would think I was smart. So it would be okay that I had sung that moron song to Morton on the sidewalk. He *was* a moron.

"Look what you're doing, Mary Ella," she said. "You're dripping."

"It's used *cars*," I said to Morton, wiping my elbows on my shorts.

"Oh," he answered. "Oh, oh, oh." He always says that when he makes a mistake, except it comes out like wo-wo-wo, as though he's talking to a horse. "Wo-wo-wo. That's what I meant. Used cars. What's a word for used cars?"

"Jalopies," I told him.

"What?"

"JALOPIES! Don't you even know what jalopies are?"

I have no idea why Morton gets to do the crossword puzzle and I don't. I'm the one who knows all about words and everything. I'm the one who knows how to spell. I'm the one who won first prize in an essay contest—not just first prize in my school, but first prize in the whole *city*. I'm the one who tells him most of the answers.

"How do you spell it?" he asked, and he put down the letters as I gave them to him. "It doesn't fit," he said. I already knew it wouldn't fit. "There are only five spaces," he said, and he rubbed at the page with an eraser worn down to its metal ring and smudged black.

I pulled the newspaper from his hand and sat down with it at the table. "Where is it, down or across?"

"Across. Where it says 'used oars.' "

"Used *cars*. CARS! There's no such thing as used oars. Can't you even read?" But then I saw that it said "used oars" after all, and I handed the puzzle back. "It's a mistake," I told him. "It's supposed to say used cars."

"Oh," he answered. "What's a word for used cars?" he asked my mother.

"I don't know, Morton. Put the puzzle away now."

"Five letters," he said.

"I don't *know!*" And then she said "Stubborn mule" into the pot.

"That doesn't fit," he said, bending over the page. "Five letters."

My mother said something else into the pot after that, but I didn't hear what it was. She wasn't really talking to the pot. She wasn't talking to herself, either. My mother doesn't talk to herself, although it looks that way. She talks to someone you can't see. Someone who moves with her from room to room and listens when she is angry at Morton. Someone who agrees with her a lot. Sometimes my mother calls Morton terrible things, but not to his face. She says them to her listener, who sits with her at the kitchen table or walks alongside her on the street and doesn't mind hearing that Morton is a stupid rat. Or brat, maybe; I can't always hear.

There was soup for dinner that night, pale-yellow soup that you could see your face in, and I blew ripples into it, making my hair dance in the bowl and my lips stretch into a broken grin. Suddenly I knew the right word for the crossword puzzle.

"I know what used oars is," I said.

"*Are,*" my father said.

"Is. It's 'rowed,'" I told Morton, waiting for him to misunderstand, to spell it wrong.

"It doesn't fit," he said, writing ROAD in the spaces.

"ROWED!" I yelled at him. "Like, he rowed a boat. Get it? He *used oars* to row the boat."

"Oh," he said. "Wo-wo-wo. How do you spell it?"

"How do you think?"

"Oh, now I know," he said, and he wrote down RODE.

"No, dummy! ROWED!" and my mother and father looked at each other across the table.

I know that look. It hangs like a little string between their faces and it means that I am smart and Morton is dumb. It means: Look at Mary Ella—three years younger and ten times smarter. It means that I make them happy and Morton doesn't, and sometimes it makes me feel good, sometimes not. That night it did.

"Put the puzzle away, Morton," my mother said. "You can finish it later."

"It *is* finished," he said. "I have to cut it out now."

That's what he does after he puts in all the S's and some words and fills the rest of the spaces with any letter at all. He cuts the puzzle out of the newspaper and adds it to his collection.

Morton collects things. He collects those little metal bottle caps with pleated edges that lie along the curb. He collects plastic spoons from lunch counters and he collects the paper sleeves from drinking straws. He used to collect the drinking straws, too, until my mother made him throw them away because of germs. He collects gum wrappers and the red cellophane strings from cigarette packs. He collects things that people throw away, and once my mother threw the *collection* away, and stuffed it into the trash can in the kitchen. "It's just a lot of rubbish," she said. "It will attract vermin," but he took it all out again and returned it to his closet. "You can come back now," I heard him say to a bottle cap. He collects things because he feels sorry for them—all those scraps and pieces lying at the curbstone or curling around the ketchup bottle on a lunchroom counter, things nobody wants.

"You can cut it out later, Morton," my mother said. "Finish your soup," but he had already gotten the scissors and was working them around the black margins on the page.

"Morton!" my father shouted, and Morton tucked the puzzle under his soup bowl. "Like a handkerchief," he said.

With my spoon I stabbed the soup in its middle, and my face broke into fragments that flew around in a circle and washed to the sides of the bowl. "My new friend just moved in," I said. "She comes from someplace far away."

"Where does she live now?" my mother asked.

"I don't know. Somewhere on the block." I put my spoon down and watched my face straighten itself out in the soup.

"No, she doesn't," Morton said suddenly. "She lives on the other block."

I looked at him. "How do *you* know?"

He was eating his soup now, and every time he put the spoon in his mouth it knocked against his back teeth. His teeth are always getting in the way. They bite into his glass when he's drinking milk and they crack against each other when he chews. I hate his teeth.

"How do *you* know?" I said again. "What other block?" It's not a good idea to ask Morton more than one question at a time. He ends up staring at you and not answering either one. "What other block?" I asked.

"Over there," he said, pointing. "Behind us."

"You mean Preston?"

"Yes," he answered. "Preston."

"How do you *know*?"

"I saw her move in," he said, and then he pushed his soup bowl away, knocking over his glass of milk, spilling it on the table, on the floor.

"Morton!" my father shouted.

"Wipe it up," my mother said in a quiet voice, not yelling. My mother is angry at Morton a lot, but she never yells and she doesn't hit him. She doesn't believe in hitting. Instead, she tells her listener about how *other* mothers would hit him if he were their child. "Any other mother," she always begins, "would take a wooden broomstick and lower it on his head." Then she talks about how lucky Morton is not to have any other mother, and after that she talks about how the trouble with her is that she's too nice. "I'm too easy on him," she says to an empty chair or to a space on the wall. "Any other mother would hit him with the morning paper." She gets very specific when she talks about what any other mother would do. *Wooden* broomstick, she says. *Morning* paper. Things like that.

Sometimes she tells about all the sacrifices she has to make for him. "All those sacrifices," she says. "The *money* I've spent on him, and the *time*. No other mother would have done as much." Long ago, when I first read about sacrifices in a mythology book, I thought the Greeks were buying lots of clothes for their kids and helping them with their schoolwork.

Meanwhile, Morton shuffles his feet around and says "tss" a lot. "Any other mother would put him in the hall closet," she said once, and I wondered why *that?* Why the *hall* closet, which has only a few coats in it and the vacuum cleaner, and really isn't such a terrible place to be? Why not their own closet, which is so small the sleeves of their clothes press into your face when you hide there and you have to stand on their shoes? Maybe that was why. Maybe she didn't want him close to her dresses, with his runny nose and all.

Morton's puzzle lay under a puddle of white, and he

stared at the swarm of bubbles that had collected in its center. *"Tss,"* he said when he finally lifted it up. The paper had turned gray and a picture from the other side showed through. *"Tss,"* he said again, and he stared at the penciled letters—the S's and the M's, soggy now and fuzzy in the tiny square rooms of their house.

Instead of being the child rabbit in my egg room that night, I was somebody else. I tied my hair into a big tail with a shoelace and I frizzed it up a lot so it would look curly. I put on two skirts, one green and long and the other yellow and short, so that together they would look like one skirt with stripes. I cut out a piece of paper and taped it to my forehead for a Band-Aid, and finally I colored my lips bright red with a lipstick that I keep behind the underwear in my drawer and that I'm not allowed to wear or even to own.

Then I made up a crazy dance: I waved my arms around a whole lot and closed my eyes, which is what Miss Frazier tells us to do in Interpretive Dance at school, and I added a folk-dance step I had learned in gym. The music was inside my head: It was the Morton-without-the-*t* song, and I sang it over and over to myself, while the giant girl watched at the window and wondered who I was.

Who *is* that? she whispered, and she pinched her fingers into a long beak, trying to seize me, to pick me up like a clothespin and dance me across the room. I whirled around faster then, and she withdrew her hand; I could hear her sigh rustle the edges of the curtains. Faster and faster I spun, until my skirts puffed out like a beach umbrella and my ponytail slapped my cheeks like a pennant in the wind. I never once looked at the window, but I felt the eye upon me all the time, and when suddenly my door flew open, I let out a small cry, thinking somehow it was the giant child, entering the egg at last. Instead it was Morton, and we stared at each other a long moment.

"Get out!" I finally screamed. "GET OUT!" and I slammed the door so hard the window, vacant now and dark, shivered in its frame.

"Mary Ella is wearing lipstick," I heard him tell my mother down the hall.

CHAPTER EIGHT

The first thing Polly noticed when I led her into my room, one week after everyone sang my song on the sidewalk, was my play orphanage. "Oh, wow, Mary Ella," she said, "these are neat," and she stared in wonder at the twenty-four little girls dressed in beautiful gowns and marching two by two across my windowsill.

They weren't real little girls. They weren't even dolls. They were the little glass bottles from the paint set I got two Christmases ago and never painted with. In fact, I never thought of them as paints at all. They had white metal heads and smooth shiny bodies and they stood side by side in their cardboard box like a row of little girls in colored gowns.

I took them out one by one that Christmas Day and arranged them in little clusters—in families, really— of purple sisters and red sisters and blue sisters, and I called them by their names. They all had beautiful names printed on labels across their stomachs: Marigold, Ecru, Heliotrope, Mauve. *Mauve!* That was the most beautiful name I had ever heard. "Hey, Mauve," I said, hopping the little bottle on the floor. "Come meet Heliotrope," and I tapped their metal heads together as they made friends.

After that they became the twenty-four girls in an orphanage. They lived in the cardboard box, standing waist high in separate round holes, and I let them out each morning just before I went to school. "Good morning, Eggshell," I'd say, standing her on the windowsill with Ebony at her side. "Good morning, Marigold. Good morning, Umber. Good morning, Violet. Good morning, Taupe," and I'd march them two by two to their classes on my desk.

The two most beautiful colors of all stood to one side, their liquid gowns as thick as syrup and flecked like a sunbeam with sparkling dust. They were the teachers, Miss Gold and Miss Silver, and they lived apart in their own waist-high spaces, square ones this time, because, unlike the orphan girls, their bodies had corners.

The school the girls all attended was just like Agnes Daly, except that they didn't have to wear uniforms, as we do, because their dresses were all different colors, and there were no boys. Everything else was the same—they had art class and Interpretive Dance and something called Free Expression, and chapel once a week.

Chapel, just like in Agnes Daly, wasn't really chapel at all. It was what other schools call assembly, and in it the orphans had to listen to the headmistress give a lecture, just like Miss Rice's, on how lucky they all were to attend such a wonderful school and to have three meals a day and good warm clothes and a roof over their heads. "Where else would it be?" Topaz once whispered to Taupe. "Under our feet?" And the headmistress punished them both, just as Miss Rice had when Iris whispered that to Rhoda. "Sit in this chair," the headmistress told her orphan girls, "and think about the consequences of offending the feelings of your fellow human beings," which is what Miss Rice had said to Rhoda and Iris that time. Then the head-mistress would talk about children on other parts of the globe—she always said globe instead of world—who wore rags and ate scraps from the street and had no roof over their heads at all.

I was the headmistress.

Each day, when the teachers entered their class-rooms, the girls would all rise. "Good *morning*, Miss Silver," they would sing together, tilting their heads forward. Or "Good *afternoon*, Miss Gold." I made that part up. We don't do that at Agnes Daly, but I wish we did.

At the end of every day the orphans would meet,

one by one, with the headmistress in her office, to discuss what they had learned.

"I learned about the Mojave Desert," Ebony would say.

"That's not the way to pronounce it, Ebony," and I would tell her how.

"Yes, Miss Briggs," she would answer, and she would repeat "Mojave" after me, saying it right.

"What did you learn about the Mojave Desert, Ebony?"

"That it's very old, and it's very dry and hot."

"That's not enough. Tomorrow you must show me where it is on the map and tell me who lives there."

"Yes, Miss Briggs," she would say.

Then I would ask Miss Gold and Miss Silver for a report on everyone's behavior. "Crimson wrote words on the mirror," Miss Gold would tell me, "and Violet spat."

I'd be very angry at that and take both girls into my office and knock their hard white heads together. I made that part up, too. Then I'd tell them they would have to stay home that night and miss the ball.

Every night there was a ball, where the girls danced to music and spun around in their lovely gowns. I would help them all get ready for it, making sure that each girl looked her best. "Let me straighten your dress," I would say to Marigold, to Indigo, to Emerald, to Mauve, and I would hold each one in my fist, shaking her gown into a shimmer, into a sheen, into a liquid glow.

Sometimes all the orphans would get sick at the same time and have to lie in a dark room, side by side, for days and days, but I would make them better. "Get better," I'd say, wetting a finger with my tongue and touching each head. "Get better," and they would, all at the same time.

Sometimes, too, they'd all get kidnapped and be taken to a cave with walls cold and green with slime, but I'd pay a huge ransom and bring them safely home.

Once in a while I would take them for a walk in town. Town was my Monopoly board, and I would move them from street to street, past the little green houses and red hotels and around the jail and the parking lot. They would all take turns walking on the boardwalk, and then I would take them to visit the poor children.

The poor children were the marbles on my Chinese checker board. There were red poor children, blue poor children, and yellow poor children; green, black, and white, and they sat in their classrooms at each point of their star-shaped school. When the rich orphans came, the poor children would look at them from their little round holes and wish they could be rich, too, with gowns of ebony, taupe, and mauve. The orphans would twirl around in front of them and talk about their parties and balls. "Too bad you can't come," they'd say, or "See how my dress sparkles in the light," like Cinderella's stepsisters, but then I would tell them to stop.

I would feel sorry for the poor children in their triangular classrooms, with their drab dresses all alike. "Stop it, Heliotrope," I'd say. "Don't talk like that." "But they're so dumb," Heliotrope would answer. "It's not nice to call people dumb," I would tell her. After that the orphan girls would not say anything at all, and I would march them all back to their house in the cardboard box.

When I couldn't think of anything else to do with them, I would call them all out of their house, one at a time, just so I could recite their beautiful names: "Vermilion? Topaz? Marigold? Mauve? Hurry up, Magenta; stop *dawdling.* Indigo? Scarlet? Taupe? *Taupe?* Where *are* you, Taupe?"

"Here, Miss Briggs."

"Why don't you ever paint anything, Mary Ella?" my mother always asked. "You have a beautiful paint set and you haven't even opened the bottles." That wasn't true. Now and then I *would* open the bottles, unscrewing the caps and peering into the liquid gowns, just as sometimes I would lift the dress of a doll to see what was underneath. But that was all. I would put their little metal heads back on and line them up again for their next class.

"I'm going to," I'd answer my mother. "I'm waiting for some good ideas of what to paint. Maybe tomorrow," but I knew I never would. Even if I had wanted to paint at home, and Morton didn't get in the way, I would never have used those paints, because by then they weren't paints at all. They were my orphan girls, and I loved them more than I loved anything in my whole life. More, even, than the Easter egg.

"Oh, wow, Mary Ella," Polly said when she saw them all lined up, two by two, on my windowsill, on their way to recess. "These are neat. Let's paint."

CHAPTER NINE

I hadn't invited Polly over. I hadn't even seen her since that day when we had all danced around Morton. She had gone away then without ever learning who I was, without saying good-bye. She didn't even know that Morton was my brother.

She wasn't my new friend at all.

When I answered the doorbell and saw her in the hall, I thought she had come to the wrong apartment, and I waited for her to notice her mistake, to say, "Oh, hey, this isn't where I wanted to be," to go up another flight of stairs, to go back down, to leave.

Kids from the block don't come to visit me very often. They don't come at all, in fact, unless I invite them, which I usually don't do. They don't especially like me, really, because I go to private school, because I'm snooty, because I have better stuff than they have, because I can never think of anything to say, because

I'm not like them. Because of Morton, too, maybe.

Once, Ina came to the door and I thought maybe she had stopped being best friends with Deirdre and wanted to be best friends with me. I asked her to come in and I began to tell her about my new Monopoly set, but she hadn't come to play with me at all. She was collecting money for heart disease and she was ringing all the doorbells in the building. I felt silly then, with the words of my invitation hanging in the doorway, so I got two dollars out of my allowance and put them in her envelope. That was all the money I had at that time, and they were the only dollar bills she had gotten. Everything else in her envelope was nickels and dimes. Some pennies.

So when Polly came to the door, I didn't say anything at all. I just waited for her to say she was looking for someone else or to ask me for money. Instead, though, she asked, "Where is everybody?"

"Where *is* everybody?" I repeated, and I looked at her for a while. "They're still in school," I finally said, and then I added, "My school's finished. I go to Agnes Daly. It's a private—"

"No, I mean here. Where's everybody here?"

"Here?" I looked at her some more. "You mean besides me?" She nodded. "My mother's at the hospital and my father's at his bookstore." I didn't mention Morton.

"What's the matter with her?" she asked, walking past me into the apartment.

"With who?"

"Your mother. How come she's in the hospital?"

"Nothing. She works there."

"Oh. Let's see your stuff," she said.

She didn't look much different from the way she had looked the week before. A Band-Aid still stretched across her forehead, and her hair was still tied together with string. Her clothes were still too long, too wrong— everything was crooked and nothing matched. I was glad of that. If she wore crazy clothes, then maybe no one else on the block would like her or want her for a friend, and she could belong to me alone.

I led her carefully through the apartment, so she could see all the things that make my building the best on the block: the metal blinds on the windows instead of paper shades, the refrigerator with a real freezer on top, the piano, and the ceiling light that turns on from a switch and not a string. "Do you want to go to the bathroom?" I asked, hoping she would, so she could see the tiles, which are pink instead of just white, and the bathtub that rests flat on the floor instead of on feet with crooked toes. It didn't matter about the clothes rack on the ceiling. Everybody around here has one of those. It's only my Agnes Daly friends who dry their clothes in secret, where no one else can see.

When we got to Morton's room, I closed the door, so she wouldn't look in and ask whose it was. So she wouldn't say after that, "Oh, I didn't know you had a *brother*," which is what the girls in school always say. "Is he cute?" So I wouldn't have to answer, "No, he's a pest. He's a big pest," which is what I always tell the girls in school, and which is what I wish he really were: a pest like everybody else's brother. "My brother's a pest, too," they answer, "but my parents like him best, anyway." They say that all the time: "My parents like my brother best," or "My parents like my sister more than me." Nobody ever says, "My parents like me best."

I never say it either, even though it's true.

It was two o'clock then. At three-thirty, Morton would be home from school, and at three I would tell Polly she had to leave. "I have to go to my piano lesson," I would tell her. Or to the dentist or to the supermarket for my mother. "So you'll have to go now."

But Polly didn't notice Morton's room at all. She didn't notice the freezer either, or the blinds or the light switch or the bathtub. All she noticed in the whole house, in fact, was my play orphanage.

"Let's paint, Mary Ella," she said. "These are neat colors. Where's the brushes?"

"I'm not sure," I said. "I don't think I have any. They're probably all—"

"Here they are," she said. "They're in this box." She had found the cardboard house where the orphan girls lived, and she was already removing the six brushes from their little elastic loops. "Oh, hey," she said, running the bristles across the back of her hand. "Feel of *that*! They're so soft, it's like they're just whispering into your skin." She had a funny way of talking. "Suh soft," she said, and "jist" for "just." "Feel of that." Where did she come from, anyway? Nobody around here talks like that.

"Let's get started," she said, placing the tip of a brush into her mouth and sucking it to a fine point.

"We can't," I said. "We can't play with those paints," and then after a while, I added, "I just got them."

I just got them. That's what Wanda or Iris or somebody like that from Calvin Boulevard says when they don't want me to play with something. "I just got them," they say.

"Can we play with these paper dolls?" I'll ask, lifting up a booklet with two punch-out girls in their underwear on the cover and pages of lovely dresses inside, and Iris or Wanda will take it away and say, "I just got them," which means no.

"I just got them," I told Polly again, but I don't think she heard me at all.

"Hey, look at this purple," she said, grabbing Violet by her neck. "Purple is my favorite color. Every time

[77]

I look at it I get this taste in my mouth, like a smooth sourball, and my ears ring, too. I hear this big fat noise. Let's start with purple, Mary Ella."

"No," I said. I took Violet back and put her in her special space in the house. "I'm really not allowed to use these paints at all. They're not mine."

"Whose are they then?"

"My mother's."

"Your *mother's*? Your mother plays with *paints*?"

"She doesn't play with them. She uses them. She's an artist."

"I thought you said she was a nurse."

"I didn't. I said she worked at the hospital."

"She's an artist at the hospital?"

"No. She does other stuff there." I was putting all the other orphan girls away now, too, as fast as I could, tumbling them down from the windowsill and cramming them into spaces that weren't their own. "She paints when she comes home," I said.

Don't worry, Emerald, I whispered in my head. *Don't worry, Taupe. Don't worry, Vermilion and Ivory. Don't worry, Marigold, Eggshell, Topaz, Mauve. I'm your headmistress, remember. Miss Briggs. I'll take care of you. Stop crying, Ebony. Remember when you were all kidnapped and I rescued you? Remember when you all got sick and I made you better? Stop crying!* I pressed Miss Gold and Miss Silver into their little square holes. *You're in charge*, I told them. *Make sure nobody worries. Especially Ebony. Look after her. She's frail*, and I pushed the roof onto their house.

"You want to play Monopoly?" I asked Polly. I slipped the orphan house under my bed. "I have this really nice set." It *is* nice. Not as nice as Wanda's, but nice just the same. Wanda has the deluxe set, with wooden houses and hotels and a real metal shoe and car to push along, while mine has just plastic things, but no one else on my block has a Monopoly set at all. "You want to play?"

"No," she said. "I don't know how. Let's paint, Mary Ella. What's your favorite color? We can do that after we do purple."

"I don't have any. And anyway, nobody calls me Mary Ella. My friends all call me M. E."

"Okay, Emmy. Let's get started."

"Not Emmy. M. E. Look," and I showed her the initials embroidered in red on my T-shirt. "See? M. E. It's my initials. For Mary Ella. Get it?"

She stared awhile at my chest. "I thought that said 'Me.'"

"No. It's M. E. It's kind of a dumb name, but everybody's called me that for years."

M. E. It would be nice to have someone call me that, I thought. "Hey, M. E.! You want to go to the movies?" "You know what, M. E.? You're the best

[79]

friend I ever had." Maybe if Polly started calling me that, other people would call me that, too. Maybe everybody would. Maybe if everybody called me M. E. I wouldn't be Mary Ella anymore. Maybe I'd be someone else. Someone everybody liked.

"Okay, Mary Ella," she said. "Where's the paper?" She was still holding the paintbrushes, and they fanned out from her fist like flowers in a vase.

"I don't have any," I told her, although that wasn't true. I had a whole stack of nice paper in my desk drawer. It had come in a special portfolio, and my mother had given it to me, along with two pens, after I won that essay contest. She thought I was going to become a famous writer—not when I grew up, but right away—and I needed a lot of paper to get started.

"It's all used up," I told Polly, but I knew she would find it anyway, and she did.

"Hey, it's right here," she said, reaching into the drawer. "Look at it all!" She held the portfolio over her head and let the paper float like leaves onto the floor. "Look at it go!" she cried. "It's like magic rugs flying around in the air. Millions of magic rugs!" The pieces came to rest in little drifts against our feet and they curled like tiny waves along the walls. "Pick as many as you want," she said, as though it were *her* paper, not mine.

She was on her hands and knees now, sliding the

orphan house out from under my bed. "Oh, wow, Mary Ella," she cried, removing the lid. "Look at this one. It glitters. *Look* at it! It's gold! Wet gold!" She began to unscrew Miss Gold's head.

"Don't do that!" I shouted, but it was too late. She had already plunged a brush into the bottle and was spreading Miss Gold's beautiful gown into a broad smear across a sheet of the paper that I was supposed to write more essays on, so I could become a famous writer someday soon.

CHAPTER TEN

The essay I won the prize for was about Elizabeth Cady Stanton, the suffragist, and I wrote it because Mrs. Pierce gave it as an assignment, not because I wanted to. Also, *I* didn't send it to the contest—my mother did. I'd never even heard of Elizabeth Cady Stanton before, and all I could find out about her in the encyclopedia was her birthday and the names of some books she had written. So I made up a lot of stuff about how if she were alive today she'd be so happy to see women voting and being lawyers and not bothering to get married. It was a terrible essay. Probably it won because nobody else had entered the contest. The prize wasn't very good either—a little medal and a certificate with my named spelled wrong: Mariella. No money. But when the letter came telling me I had won, my mother got all excited and called up all her friends, reciting the name of the award very carefully: The Francis Bacon Essay Society Award, as though it were the Nobel Prize or something, and she had won it herself.

The medal was attached to a little purple-and-yellow ribbon, the kind with ridges to bump your fingernail along, and it was engraved with my initials—M. B.—and the date. It came in a little box with fuzzy cardboard that was supposed to look like velvet, and it lies, with the certificate and a newspaper clipping—where my name is also spelled wrong—in my mother's bureau drawer, not mine.

"This is a crummy color," Polly said, tilting her head to one side as she examined the stripe she had just painted on my writing paper. "It isn't gold at all. It's mud. They put mud in this bottle and made it look like gold."

She was right. It *was* the color of mud. Outside Miss Gold's glass body, the paint had no shine at all, and the sunbeam flecks lost their glint. Mud and bits of grit was what it was like. I looked at Miss Gold standing on the floor with her head off and her dress dripping down around her neck, and I reached out for her. *Miss Mud,* I said, tightening her head back on and wiping her shoulders with my thumb. What would the orphan girls sing out now, I wondered, when she entered their room? Good *morning,* Miss Mud, probably, and Vermilion would laugh. *Shut up, Vermilion,* I said in my head.

"Watch this now," Polly said, and she began to pull all the orphans out of their holes and to drop them in a heap on her lap.

"Stop that!" I yelled. "STOP THAT! Put them back in their house! Box, I mean. Put them back in their *box!*" But she moved away from me and began scrambling the orphans all around, knocking their bodies together as she searched for something. Finally she found what she wanted, and she put Violet's head between her teeth and twisted it off. "I'm starting with purple," she said.

"No, you're not!" I pulled Violet away and screwed her head back on.

"Red, then," she said, picking up Vermilion. "You want to see something?" She undid Vermilion's head and stirred her dress around with a paintbrush.

"No! No, I don't. I don't want to see something. I want to see you put that back. That's what I want to see." My teachers in school talk like that, and I talked like that, too, sometimes, to the little orphans when they said fresh things. "*Stop* that!" I yelled. "You're ruining her *dress!*"

"Ready? Watch." She folded down the top joint of her thumb, and on its smooth, shiny knuckle painted a little red face, with O's for eyes, an L for a nose, and a shallow U for a smile. "Now look," and she straightened out her thumb, wrinkling the skin into the face

[84]

of an old man, a monkey, a bulldog, a crying baby—
a what? I couldn't tell. Something ugly. The next
instant she smoothed it out again and it smiled up at
me like a face on a balloon.

"Don't do that!" I yelled again, and I grabbed Vermilion from her hand, spilling some of her red dress
on my wrist. "Look what you did! She's getting all
messed up!" I put Vermilion's head back on. *Stop
squealing*, I whispered to her. *Your dress just got a little
torn around the shoulders. It's okay. Don't worry about
it. I'll make it better. I'll fix it.* "This stuff costs a lot of
money," I told Polly. "Wait till my mother comes
home. She's going to be really mad."

"Look," she said. "Now I'll do a green one," and
she dipped the same brush, still dripping with the red
of Vermilion's dress, into Emerald's satin gown.

I tried to grab her arm this time, but she was too
quick. A scarlet swirl floated for a long moment on
the green surface like a goldfish in a pond. "Don't," I
said, watching now as the red spread and darkened to
gray, to brown, to black, but my voice was so tight I
could barely hear it myself.

I watched in silence after that as Polly painted the
knuckles on all her other fingers with the dresses of
my orphan girls—of Marigold, Ebony, Indigo, Taupe,
mixing them up, streaking them in their glass bodies:
black on blue, yellow on red, green on white.

[*85*]

"Now I'll do yours," she said, squeezing my hands into fists and making little features on each of my knuckles with the colors of ten different girls. I tried at first to twist away, but her hold was hard, and I finally sat still, offering my hand quietly, as I do in the school infirmary when the nurse bandages a cut.

Be still, Sapphire, I said. Listen to me, Topaz. Listen to me, all of you. I have something to say. This is a dream that you're having, okay? It's a terrible dream that you're all having at the same time. Pretty soon it will be morning and you'll wake up and see that it was all a bad dream. But I wondered what I would tell them the next day when they saw that their gowns were still streaked with crazy colors and torn at the shoulders and neck.

"Now," Polly said, raising first her right fist and then her left. "This hand is the boys and this one is the girls. Look, they're kissing," and she brought her two rows of knuckles together so that their painted lips touched. "Now let's give them names. Boys first. The thumb is Tony, and the others are Donald, Angel, George, and Max."

How did she think those names up so fast? I wondered. Angel. *Angel!* Max. It used to take me weeks to name my dolls, when I played with dolls, and even then I'd never be sure I had chosen the right ones. Fancy names they would be, out of books, mostly—

Daphne and Belinda, things like that—and then I'd keep them all secret, because they sounded dumb when I spoke them aloud. "What is your dolly named?" my mother's friends would ask, and I would answer, "Sally."

"What're yours named?" Polly asked. "Start with the girls."

I peered into the little faces smiling at me and then frowning as I smoothed and shriveled my skin. Maybe, I thought, *they* could be my orphan girls—these little painted faces on my hands. Maybe they would stick to my knuckles forever, and would trail alongside me wherever I went. Ten little orphan girls lined up in rows, smiling and frowning at home and at school. They would go to Agnes Daly instead of the classroom on my desk, and they would learn about the Mojave Desert from Mrs. Pierce instead of from Miss Silver and Miss Gold. For recess they would curl around the jungle-gym bars and for chapel they would listen to Miss Rice. At night they would still go to lovely balls, creating their own music as they ran up and down the piano keys, and later they would sleep among the folds of my pajama sleeves instead of in the circles of a cardboard box. Maybe it would be better if they were fingers instead of bottles of paint. For them, for me.

"Give them names," Polly said.

"Okay," I answered. "This one is Heliotrope," and

I touched the purple-blue face on my thumb. "And this one is Topaz."

"*What?*"

"Heliotrope and Topaz. And these are Marigold and Umber and Eggshell."

Polly stared at me. "What kind of names are those? Toe pads? Eggshell? *Eggshell?* You can't name anybody that. Pick a real name."

"I can't think of one," I said.

"Yes, you can. Everybody can think of a name."

"Sally," I said, straightening out my thumb and staring into its old, wrinkled face. "This one's Sally." After that I picked names of kids from my class at school. "This one's Rhoda," I said, "and this one's Iris."

"Okay," she said when they were all named. "Let's play that they're gangs."

"Gangs?"

"Yeah. My gang against your gang," and she suddenly pressed her knuckles so hard against mine I let out a cry.

"Who was that?" she asked. "Which one cried?"

I looked at the row of faces smiling up at me from my hand. "Sally," I said. "She always cries," and I pressed back, crushing the smooth little smiles on Polly's fingers.

The two gangs fought for a long time after that, boys against boys, girls against girls, their faces all smiles when they tightened for a blow, wrinkled into frowns when they stopped.

"Let's do knees next," Polly said, pausing for a moment. "Me first," and she rubbed a paintbrush on the inside of Sapphire's neck.

Stop it, I yelled at Sapphire in my head. *Stop crying like that. And you, too, Taupe. Stop crying, all of you! Ebony! Umber! Be still,* and I closed my eyes because I didn't want to look at them, because their heads were knocked off, because their gowns were in shreds, because they were, in fact, no longer orphan girls at all; they were ordinary bottles of paint, with streaks of color hardening down their sides and collecting in the ridges of their necks.

It hurt, banging our knees into each other, but neither of us cried out. I tightened my hands into fists when our bones were set to strike, and the little knuckle faces smiled with every blow.

"Hey," Polly said. "Look what you just did when you wiped your face. You made a green face on your nose!" and she pushed me in front of the mirror. "Scrunch it up and make it holler."

I stared hard at my reflection. Streaks of color spread across my cheeks like the patterns on a cow, forming no design, but the three green spots on my nose made a perfect face: an eye, an eye, and a mouth. I wrinkled them into a scowl.

"Oh, wow," Polly said, and she painted a face on her nose, too. "Watch *this*."

We stood side by side after that, stretching our lips, pulling our cheeks, making faces on top of our faces, and staring at them in the mirror. We looked funny like that, and suddenly I thought: This is what best friends do. I bet this is what Ina and Deirdre do when they play together, and Iris and Rhoda, too. This is what it's like to have a best friend, and I looked again at our faces in the mirror and began to laugh. Big laughs burst from my mouth, taking me by surprise. Real laughs, the kind that come from your stomach somewhere and that you can't help—not those little laughs that you make up when somebody tells a joke that you don't get. Laughs with tears, even; little rivers of water began to spread around my eyes and turn purple as they hit my painted cheeks.

Purple laugh tears. They were my first laugh tears ever, and I blotted them onto a tissue. I stared into the soft, wide splotches that they made. Polly was right, purple did have a taste—I could feel its sudden smoothness on the edges of my tongue—and it had a sound, too—deep, like the gong Miss Rice strikes at the start of every chapel when she wants us to be silent and think important thoughts.

Later, when Polly wasn't looking, I folded the tissue over its own purple dampness and put it into my dresser drawer, to keep. I had never laughed like that before, and I thought it really didn't matter that I didn't have my orphan girls anymore. Polly was going to be my best friend.

"Let's do our elbows," I said, out of breath. "Let's paint them all the colors in my whole paint set." I had just dipped a brush into a bottle of blue when somebody said, "What are you doing?" and we both turned around.

Morton was standing in the doorway.

CHAPTER ELEVEN

He looked as dumb as ever.

My mother always makes Morton wear his door key on a shoelace around his neck, and the lace was in his mouth now, stretching from ear to ear like a thin white grin. Also, his shoes were untied. *Shoes!* Morton wears real shoes all the time, even to school, even in the summer, although he has perfectly good sneakers. "I'm keeping my sneakers for when I have to climb something," he always said. "Climb what?" I'd ask, and he'd answer, "I don't know. Maybe a fence."

His Mickey Mouse shirt was tucked inside his underpants, so that a band of gray elastic showed above his belt, and sticking out from the elastic was a long white envelope.

"What are *you* doing here?" I demanded. I could still pretend he wasn't my brother. I could say he lived downstairs and had come up to play with my things. Or he got the apartments mixed up and wandered into mine by mistake. Or he was the delivery boy, bringing groceries. Something.

"What?" he asked, staring at me.

"What are you *doing* here?" What *was* he doing there, anyway? It wasn't even three o'clock yet and he never got home before three-thirty. Then I remembered—today was the last day of school. The last Friday of June. That was why he was home early, and that was why he had an envelope. It contained his report card.

"I don't know," he answered. "I'm just here. Where's Mom?"

"Who?"

"Mom."

"I don't know," I said. "I don't know where your mother is. Why don't you go away where you belong? I don't have time for you. I'm playing with my friend now."

He looked at me the way he always does when he doesn't understand—his eyes stayed the same but his lips got puffy. I put my face up to his. "I said, why don't you go *away* now," and he did. He walked into his room, tripping on his shoes as he went and chewing hard on the shoelace in his mouth.

I turned to Polly and shrugged at her so she, too, would wonder what Morton was doing at my door, but she brushed past me and followed him down the hall.

"Hey, Morton," she said, "come here. I want to ask you something," and I suddenly remembered her words of the week before: *Hey, Morton. Come here. I want to ask you something.* And then, when he crossed the street, *Is that your girlfriend?*

That's what she still thought—Morton was my boyfriend, not my brother. My *boyfriend!* And he had come to my apartment to be with me, to talk to me, to play, to—whatever boyfriends do.

"Polly!" I called after her. "*Polly!* Wait! I have to tell you something," although I didn't know what I would tell her. "Polly, come *here.*"

"Morton," she repeated, "I want to ask you a question," and then I thought of something else. Maybe she really didn't care who Morton was. Maybe she didn't care if he was my boyfriend or my brother or anything. Maybe she just saw him there and decided to play a trick on him, which is what everybody does when they see Morton. "Hey, Morton, come here," they say, just as Polly had. "I want to ask you something." Or tell.

"Hey, Morton," Ezra will suddenly call from down the block. "Come here. I want to tell you something. It's a secret," and he'll blow a whistle into Morton's ear.

"Hey, Morton, come here. I want to tell you something. Shake," and a hand will reach out to buzz a little shock into Morton's palm.

"Hey, Morton, come here. You know what?" This was the longest trick of all. "There was a guy around here from Western Union. He had a telegram for someone named Morton Briggs who lived in your building, but I told him there was no one there by that name."

Morton stared at him for a long time. "That's me," he finally said. "Morton Briggs."

"It is? That's your name? I thought it was Morton Diggs or something. Anyway, when I told him there was nobody around here named that he just tore the telegram up. It was something about winning a lot of money."

I never say anything when somebody plays a trick on Morton. I just stand and watch, waiting for it to be over.

Sometimes I play tricks on him myself.

"Come here," Polly said. "I want to ask you something."

Morton turned around. "What?" he said.

Don't play a trick, I said to myself. *Don't, don't, don't. Best friends don't play tricks on each other's brothers.*

"Where are your trains?" she asked.

"My trains?"

"Yeah, the electric ones. With the station and all. Where are they?"

His trains? His train set? How did she know about *that?* . . . *Nobody* knew about Morton's train. What kind of trick was this, anyway? Morton's train set had lain under his bed in its big flat box for more than a year. Nobody had touched it since the time Lenny from his class had come over that day long ago and played for a whole afternoon, all by himself, while Morton watched from the sofa. "What train?" I asked. "How do you know about his train?"

"He told me," she said.

"Who? Lenny?"

"No, *him.* Your brother."

"What brother?"

"How many do you have? That one. Morton."

"Morton told you about his train? When did he tell you that?" How did she know he was my brother?

"When he came to my house."

I stared at her. What *was* this, anyway? "Morton came to your house?" I turned to him. "You went to her house? When did you go there? How come you never said so?" My voice was growing loud and high. "What were you doing at her house?" *When she's supposed to be* my *friend,* I thought.

"It's not her house," he answered. "It's her grandma's." He slipped his report card out from his belt and propped it up on his dresser, in front of the clock. His name had been written on the envelope in fancy script, with extra tails dangling from the capital letters and little g's that looked like 8's. The kind I always try to copy, but can't do right. "She lives with her grandma," he added.

"I know that," I said, although I didn't. "I know she lives with her grandmother. When did you go there? What were you doing? What was he doing at your house?" I said to Polly.

"Playing," she answered.

"Playing what?"

"Dress-up."

"She showed me her grandma's clothes," Morton said. "We tried them on."

I stared at him. "You tried them *on?* You played dress-up in her grandmother's clothes? At *your age?*"

"She had a whole bunch of hats," Morton said. "And shoes that you needed a hook to put them on, like long ago."

I turned to Polly to see if she was laughing, but she wasn't even listening. "Where are they, Morton?" she asked. "The trains with the station?"

Morton pulled the train box out from under his bed and turned it upside down. "Hey, look out!" I cried, as a rush of silver track crashed around his legs and train cars slid about like little mice.

"Is this it?" Polly had the transformer in her hands. "Is this the station?"

"No," Morton told her. "That's the thing with wires you attach. *This* is the station." He held up a little plastic platform with a tiny slatted bench and sign-boards at the edges of the roof. ORCHARDTOWN, they read. "That's the name of the town where the train goes," Morton explained. "Look." He balanced the station on his knees. "This is Orchardtown, and my legs are all the streets," and he laughed his dumb laugh.

"Look at *this*," I said quickly, before he could say any more dumb things, and I held up the transformer. "This is where they keep all the volts and watts. I can explain how it works, if you want. I can show you how to set it all up with the wires. I know all about how to do it. It's really very complicated. You have to do it just right or it won't work. You need a scientific mind to figure it out," I added. "My teacher is always telling me I have a scientific mind." She isn't really. She says Iris and Joseph have scientific minds. I have a literary mind.

"Let's see the station, Morton," Polly said, holding out her hand. "Let's *see* it," and I finally understood what her trick was going to be. "Let's see it" is what everybody says to Morton when they want to take his stuff away and keep it for themselves. "Let's see it," they say, and he gives them whatever is in his hands or his pockets. For good.

"Let's see your money," Ezra said one morning, a long time ago, as Morton and I stood beneath the awning.

"What?" Morton asked, blinking a little.

"Your *money*. You know, money? Coins? Round silver things? You buy stuff with it?" He was wearing a pair of mirrored sunglasses, even though it was winter, and our whole street, tiny as a peep show, lay inside their lenses—the sidewalk, the cars at the curb, the awning frame, Morton, me. Two whole streets, really—one at each eye. Everything was double; I raised my arm in a brief wave, and two small snowsuit arms waved back. "Let's see your money, Morton," he said, turning the double street from side to side.

"Wo-wo-wo-wo-wo," Morton said, catching on, and he groped about in his pocket for the two quarters from his allowance.

"Let's *see* them," Ezra said, putting his hand out.

Morton held up the two coins by their rims and turned them back to front. "See?" he said.

"Very funny," Ezra said. His hand was still out.

Finally I spoke up. "He doesn't mean *look* at, dummy," I said to Morton. "He means *hold*," and I looked over to Ezra and smiled. I wanted him to know that I wasn't dumb like my brother. I wanted him to know that just because I had a dumb brother, that didn't mean I was dumb, too. "He means give them to him," I said, and I plucked the two quarters from Morton's fingers and handed them over, waiting for Ezra to say something nice to me.

"Thanks," is what he said. He tossed the quarters one at a time into the air and slapped them on the back of his other hand. "Thanks a lot," and he disappeared around the corner, taking the whole street in his sunglasses along with him. Double: double Morton, double awning frame, double sidewalk, double cars, double me.

After that, Morton understood what "Let's see it" meant, so that one day when some kid no one had ever seen before came up to him and said, "Let's see your bicycle," Morton just gave it to him.

"Why'd you do that, Morton?" Franklin had asked. "Why'd you let him ride it, anyway?"

"What?"

"Why'd you let him get on your bike like that and just ride it away? You didn't even *know* him," he said. "He just *took* it. He took your bike and you let him. You just *let* him."

Morton pressed the palms of his hands together and spun them around each other, making one finger wiggle up and the other down, like a clapper toy that you shake on New Year's Eve. He had just learned that trick and he did it all the time. "Look," he'd say, wiggling his fingers in my mother's face. "A bird." Once he scratched her eye doing that.

"Why'd you let him?" Franklin insisted.

"He wanted to see it," Morton explained.

And now Polly.

"Let's see it," she said, reaching for the little plastic station on Morton's knee.

"No!" I shouted. "It's Morton's!" But he gave it to her, anyway.

"Look," she whispered, stroking the roof as though it were some kind of pet animal. "Look at the little signs with the name of the town on them." She flicked them with her fingernail and made them swing. "And the billboards. Look how tiny." She was like the giant girl at the window of my egg room. "And the little bench," she went on.

"You could sit on it if you wanted," Morton said, "and wait for the train to come."

"Yeah, sure," I said, and I smiled so Polly would think Morton was just making a joke.

"You could grow down to be small," he went on, "and then when the train came you could get on. You could have a little ticket, too, to give to the con-ductor."

"You want to see how the train can go?" I asked Polly. "I can show you how," but she didn't hear me. She was listening to Morton.

"I could be the conductor," he said. "I could get small, too, and wear a blue uniform with a cap to put on my head. All aboard!" He waved his hand back and forth. "All aboard, everybody! We're going to Africa!"

I waited for Polly to laugh, to say that was dumb—you can't take a train to Africa—but she just stroked the roof some more and finally, after a long while, she placed the station very carefully on Morton's knee.

"Or Australia, maybe," she said, and I stared first at her and then at Morton.

CHAPTER TWELVE

When Morton first got his electric train, I didn't believe it was his. I thought it was for me.

It was lying in an enormous box on the coffee table one evening when I returned home from visiting Wanda, and Morton and my mother and father were all looking down at it as though it were a new baby.

"What's that?" I asked, and Morton moved aside so I could see. My breath caught in my throat for a moment. "Oh, wow," I whispered. It didn't seem to belong in our living room; it was too new, too wonderful, with the tracks in perfect stacks of silver arcs, and the cars all gleaming in a row. "Oh, neat," I said, and neat is what I meant—the *tidy* kind of neat, where everything is in its own special place.

"There's a light in the engine that goes on," Morton told me, "and pills to make smoke."

I lifted up a little car and stood it on my palm. It was the color of a buttercup, and bright-red letters spelled a name on either side: Chesapeake & Ohio, they read, beneath the drawing of a cat. I skidded the wheels against my arms and watched as they spun on and on. "It looks so real," I whispered, stopping the wheels all at once with a finger. *Everything* looked real. The doors on the boxcars slid back and forth, and the windows on the passenger cars were thin and clear. A tunnel made to look like brick and stone stood in one side of the box, the little plastic station in the other. ORCHARDTOWN, said the letters on its signs.

"It's beautiful," I whispered.

"It's for me," Morton said, and I stared at him.

"Is that true?" I asked, turning first to my mother and then to my father. "Is that *true*? This is for *him*?"

"We got you a writing set," my mother answered. "Let me show it to you. A lovely writing set in a portfolio, with special paper and two gold pens. Because you won the essay contest," she added, and she handed me a thin package wrapped in pink.

I opened it on the sofa, where I could still look at the train set, and I dropped all the wrappings at my feet. The special paper wasn't really that great. It didn't have lines on it, and it wasn't for writing essays at all. It was for writing letters, and it came with matching envelopes and a little address book. And the pens were gold *colored*.

"It's very nice," I said, closing the portfolio on my knee. I still couldn't believe it. *I* won the essay contest, and all I got was a bunch of paper, that you couldn't even write an essay on, and a couple of pens? While Morton got the most wonderful train set in the whole world? With pellets to make smoke and a real light bulb in the nose of the engine? *Morton?*

He *never* got presents better than mine. Never. At Christmas we always got one present each, and mine was always better. The year I got my Monopoly set he got a bedspread, and when I got my paint set all he got was gloves and a scarf. Stuff he needed anyway.

I looked into the train box and then up to my mother. "It's not even his birthday," I said. "How come he got that?"

"He's never had a train set before," she answered.

"So?" Neither had I.

He wouldn't even know how to use it, I thought. He wouldn't know how to attach the wires to make it go. He wouldn't know how to put the tracks together to make a circle. He wouldn't know how to plug it *in*. He wouldn't even like it.

It was a while before he touched anything in the box, and when he did it was only to lift out two pieces of track and try to fit them together. They got stuck halfway, and when he pulled them apart, one of them bent. *"Morton!"* my father shouted, and my mother whispered something to the lamp.

"Here, Morton," I said. "I'll show you how," and I unpacked all the pieces of track and spread them out on the floor. There were curved pieces and straight pieces and double pieces that made X's and Y's. The picture on the lid showed a huge figure eight inside an oval, with a siding leading off from one edge, and I began to copy it, piece by piece. "Look," I explained to him. "It's easy. You start with this piece that looks like an X, and then you add all the other pieces until it's like the one on the picture."

Meanwhile, my mother and father were connecting wires from the transformer to a little metal plate and moving the sofa so they could reach the outlet on the wall. Morton sat on a chair the whole time and watched. "It looks good," he said, when everything was all set up. "It looks very good," and it did. It looked wonderful.

I had hooked all the train cars together and placed them exactly in front of the platform, so passengers could step right onto the cars without falling, and I had set up the tunnel on the other side, halfway through the train's journey. The track covered almost all the living-room rug, and parts of it ran in and out of the legs of tables and chairs. When I narrowed my eyes I saw a real countryside, with a long silver track running through fields of flattened flowers and trees of dark-stained wood.

"Make it go," Morton said, and he leaned forward in his chair. "Make it go fast," and I turned on the switch.

The bulb on the engine turned a quick, sharp white, and a motor hummed. The train moved slowly at first, pulling itself carefully away from the platform, but it picked up speed after that and worked its way along the tracks, in, out, around—in, out, around—through the tunnel, out. None of us spoke. Suddenly I turned the speed dial as far as it would go, and the train flew around in crazy loops, so fast I could no longer read the letters on the cars. Banners of smoke burst from the chimney and a sudden whistle sounded—whispery, low, and full of warning.

Finally I drew it to a stop, and lowered two fingers onto the roof of a car. They were the new passengers, going to their grandmother's house, and they'd never been aboard a train before today. In and out they went, in and out, past some cows, a pond, a windmill, a school, the house where their grandmother waited at the door. "We're here!" one of them shouted.

"Give Morton a turn now," my mother said. "It's his train, after all."

"Oh, sure," I said, pulling the passengers away and turning off the switch. "Here, Morton. It's your train. *Here,*" and before my mother or father could say anything, I pulled all the tracks apart and scrambled them around on the rug. "It's all yours," I said, and I disconnected the train cars, too. "Now you can put it together all by yourself. Go ahead, Morton. Go *ahead.* Just copy the picture on the box. It's easy. Look, you can make a siding and everything," I added, knowing he didn't even know what a siding was. "Anybody can do it. A baby, even."

He picked up two pieces of track and carefully fitted them together, nicely this time. "That's fine, Morton," my mother said. Then he added more pieces, and some more after that, making a crazy zigzag that wandered all over the living-room floor and didn't join together end to end. Finally he picked up the yellow car with the red writing on it and tried to run it along one of the curves, but its wheels kept sliding off the track, and after that he just pushed it up and down his outstretched arm.

"*Rum-rum-rum,*" he said, while the wheels slid silently along his sleeve, "*rum-rum-rum,*" and my mother and my father exchanged that look.

I carried my new writing set into my room and drew out the top sheet of paper. "Stupid brat," I wrote with one of the gold-colored pens. "Stupid brat, stupid rat, stupid brat," I wrote, but not with the writing end. With the other end, so no one could see—no one but some private reader, invisible and silent as the listener who always sat by my mother's side and agreed with her whispered words.

CHAPTER THIRTEEN

Two weeks after Morton got his train set, I found out why he had been given it in the first place.

"Morton," my mother said to him one morning, "why don't you ask one of the boys in your class to come over and play with you sometime? You never invite anyone home. Why is that? You have a nice train set now," she said, "and lots of boys would like to play with it. I bet no one in your class has a train as nice as that."

And that was why: He had been given the train set so he could make friends, and every day after that, when Morton came home from school, my mother would ask, "Morton, did you ask one of the boys to come and play with your train?" and he would say no, he forgot.

In the end, though, someone did come.

Not because *Morton* invited him, but because my mother did. We were all walking back from the supermarket one afternoon, and Morton was pulling the grocery cart, when some boy passed and said hello to him. "The boy said hello," my mother said, and she offered the smile that Morton didn't give. The next minute she was calling him back and telling him about Morton's new train set and asking him to visit, while Morton pulled the groceries up the street.

My mother does things like that. Even with me. When we go to the beach in the summer, she always finds some girl my age and brings her over to me. "I found a nice girl for you to play with," she says, and all of a sudden I am looking into the face of someone I will hate. Someone in a bathing suit that is either a whole lot nicer than mine or a whole lot worse. "Her name is Amanda and she's just your age," my mother says, and she waits for me to smile, to say hello, to be friendly, to be liked, to be not the same as Morton.

"Come tomorrow afternoon," she said to the boy on the sidewalk, and I hoped that when he said no he would offer a really good reason. Not just "No, I have a lot of work to do," but "No, I'm moving away," or "No, I have to get my appendix out." Instead, he said yes.

When we opened the train box the next afternoon, we found a dead moth lying in the corner. Morton lifted it up and looked at it, and then settled it carefully in the bottom of the yellow car. It was a passenger, he said. It was Mr. Moth and he was going to work. "Mr. Moth is going to his bookstore."

Lenny looked at him for a while. "What do you want that for?" he asked "What do you want with a dead bug in the coal car?" He pinched its body between two fingers and blew the silver dust into the air.

"*Tss*," Morton said, and then he picked up the little car and held it out. "You want to see something? You want to see what I can do?"

"Wait," I said, so Morton wouldn't make the car go rum-rum-rum on his arm in front of this new boy. "I need that!" But Morton didn't answer. "Look," he said, and he wheeled the car up the length of his arm and down again. "*Rum-rum-rum*," he said, and then he let it roll down his thigh.

Lenny took the car from Morton and attached it to the engine. "You want to know what gauge this train is?" I asked him.

"I already know," he said. "It's H-O. Where can we set it up?"

"On the rug," I answered. "I'll show you how."

My mother had told me to be in charge until she came home. "You're the hostess, Mary Ella," she had said that morning. I was to serve cookies and milk when they came in after school, and then help set up the train. "And then go to your room. Lenny isn't coming to play with you," she said. "He's coming to play with Morton," although that wasn't true; he was coming to play with the train.

I set out the cookies and milk on the coffee table. My mother had baked the cookies herself, for Morton and his new friend, and they were very fancy, like holiday cookies, with different shapes and colored icing and sugar sparkles, even. Too fancy, really. I messed them around a little to make them look plain.

"I'll set the tracks up now," I said, and I took them all out of the box. "I can make them look just like the ones on the cover. You want to see? You start with this X piece, and then you make a figure eight, and after that—"

"Never mind," Lenny said. "I can do it myself." He knelt on the rug and slipped all the track pieces together, one after another, without even checking the picture on the lid. He was finished in two minutes.

"You want me to show you how to attach all the wires?" I asked.

"No," he answered, setting up the transformer. "I can do that, too."

When he had all the cars hooked up and in place on the track, I told him about the smoke pellets for the engine. "They make real smoke," I said, "and the engine lights up and blows a whistle."

"I know," he answered.

After that I stood aside and watched him play with

Morton's train. Morton watched, too, from the sofa. He had taken a glass of milk and was drinking it as he always did, lifting the bottom too quickly so that a wave of liquid washed over his upper lip, leaving a stripe, and swallowing with the noise of a frog.

"I'm going to my room now," I said. "Let me know if you need anything," but neither one of them answered.

I sat alone on my bed for a long time after that, listening to the hum of the train motor and the rustle of wheels on tracks. Now and then there was the sound of Lenny's voice. "Is there anything to eat besides these cookies?" he asked once, and then, later, "What other stuff do you have?" I heard their footsteps go into Morton's room and, soon after, the rattle of things in boxes—puzzle pieces, probably, or wooden Bingo numbers. Later, a rush of something spilling on the floor.

"Don't you have anything else?" I heard, and finally, "Is this all?" There was silence for a while, and then came Morton's voice. "You want to see something else?" he said. "Something really nice?" and once again I followed the sound of their footsteps.

This time they led to my mother and father's room, and I sat up straight and still on my bed. A drawer slid open, and there was silence. He's showing Lenny her jewelry, I suddenly thought. He's showing him the string of pale-pink beads that used to be her grand-mother's and her good earrings with the tiny specks of sapphire. He's going to show him the bracelet with the green stones and the cameo pin that has a carving of a lady with peach-colored hair. Lenny's going to look at it all and then he's going to say, "Hey, let's see that. Let's just see that stuff," and he's going to slip it all into his pocket and go home. I ran out of my room and down the hall.

"Get out of there!" I yelled. "What do you think you're doing in here? GET OUT OF THEIR *ROOM!*" And then I stopped still. Both boys were bent over an open drawer, and Morton was showing Lenny my box of prize essay things: the certificate in its fake leather folder, the newspaper clipping and, pinched between his fingers like a struggling butterfly, the little silver medal on its gold-and-purple ribbon.

"My sister won this," he was saying.

"Get out of there," I said again, but this time my voice was just a whisper, and I don't think they heard me at all.

CHAPTER FOURTEEN

Lenny never came back, and the train set had lain under Morton's bed ever since. Sometimes my mother would threaten to give it away, but she never did. "It's a shame," she would say, hitting the box unexpectedly with the vacuum cleaner brush. "Such a nice train set and nobody ever touches it. Why don't we give it to someone who would appreciate it, instead of leaving it on the floor week after week, collecting dust?"

Sometimes I thought that in some strange way she was *glad* that he never played with his train, that he didn't know how, that no friends came. So she could be angry.

"Collecting dust?" Morton asked. "The train collects dust?"

"Not that kind of collect," I told him quickly. "Not like collecting bottle caps. She means it gets dusty."

"I'm sure there are lots of boys who would be glad

to have a train set like that," she would go on. She is always saying how everybody would be glad to do things. And then she would say she was going to speak to his teacher. "Miss Carroll probably knows of some poor boy who could use a good train set. I'll have to go in someday and ask her."

Then Morton would say he was going to start playing with his train very soon. "Tomorrow, maybe," but he never did.

"Why don't you give it to me?" I asked her once. "I know how to play with it. I know all about what gauge it is and everything, and how to make figure eights," but she didn't answer, and the train remained under Morton's bed, collecting dust.

Until the day Polly came.

"You want to see how it can go?" I asked her again. "You want me to make it run? Sit up on the bed and I'll show you. Look. This is the track," I said, laying all the pieces out on the floor, "and these are the cars. The doors really open and the windows are made of glass. It's H-O," I added. "That's the gauge," and I waited for her to say, "What's that, gauge?" but she didn't say anything at all. "This is the engine," I told her. I dropped a little pellet into the chimney, but not so she could see—secretly, so she would be surprised when it suddenly began to smoke. "And here's how to work the transformer." I fastened all the wires together, making them look more complicated than they really were.

"Now watch." I felt like a magician about to put on a show. "I can make the train go wherever I tell it to. Ready?" I turned on the switch, and with my fingers on the dial, I gave it commands: *Go here, go there. Cross over. Go inside. Go outside. Go fast.* It was nice doing that, making the train follow my orders while Polly watched from the bed. "Look at the smoke!" I cried, as soft puffs of white lifted into the air. I twisted the dial all the way to the right and the cars flew around and around and in and out, and then I brought them to a perfect stop, exactly in front of the station. "Everybody off!" I said. "Last stop!" I turned to Polly. "Isn't that wonderful? Isn't that the best train you've ever seen?" I asked, although I knew it was probably the *only* train she'd ever seen.

"That's it?" she said. "That's all it can do? Just go in and out like that, and around?"

"I can make it do something," Morton said. "You want to see?"

"Don't do that, Morton," I told him. "That's bad for the wheels," but he didn't listen. He removed the train from the track and unhitched the little yellow coal car. "Watch this," he said. "Watch what I can do." He curled the fingers of his left hand into a fist and stretched out his arm to make a track. Then he ran the little car along his vein, back and forth, back and forth. *"Rum-rum-rum,"* he said.

"You'll ruin it," I said, "doing that."

"Look what else," he said. "Watch out, Mary Ella. Watch out of the way."

I didn't move.

"Move back, Mary Ella. I want to do something. Mary Ella?"

"What?" I finally said, as though I were just waking up. "Oh, are you talking to me? How come you're calling me *that*? You know nobody's called me Mary Ella in years."

He stared at me.

"M. E.," I told him.

He stared at me some more and then he said, "Wo-wo-wo-wo-wo. I forgot."

"I don't even answer to Mary Ella anymore," I explained to Polly. "Nobody calls me that at all."

"Ina does," she said.

"Move out of the way, Mary Ella," Morton said. "I want to show how I can do something," and this time I moved.

He sent the coal car crashing down the ramp of his thighs and onto the floor. Polly laughed. "Let me try that," she said, and she rolled it down her thighs, too. "Neat," she said. "This is really neat. Now watch *this*."

She ran the car along the floor, as though it were a piece of chalk, and then up Morton's bed, onto its spread, over the headboard, up the wall, around the picture, across the radiator, and back along the floor to its box. *"Rum-rum-rum,"* she said, and she rolled it over to Morton.

"Rum-rum-rum," he said, sending it back. *"Rum-rum-rum,"* they said together, rolling the car into each other's knees.

I stared at them both. What was happening here, anyway? Morton was the dumbest kid on the block, and the ugliest, too. He even had a dumb name, and here was Polly playing with him as though she actually *liked* him—going rum-rum-rum with him and everything, and listening to all that stuff about Africa. He'd even been to her house once—when?—and played dress-up. What was the *matter* with her?

She was looping the coal car through the air now. "Watch it go!" she cried. "It's a bat!" I wondered suddenly what my mother would say if she came in at that moment and saw what had happened now that someone had finally come again to play with Morton's train. She'd be home soon, I thought, and I glanced up at the clock on the dresser, but instead of its face I saw the flat white envelope that held, like a secret message, Morton's seventh-grade report card.

"What's in the envelope?" Polly asked, following my eyes.

"My report card," Morton answered.

"Your report card? What did you get?"

"O," he said. "I got O in conduct."

"What's that stand for, O?"

"Outstanding," he told her. "I got outstanding in conduct. Because I'm good."

Morton always gets O in conduct, and instead of being happy about that, my mother gets angry. "I can never understand," she says to her listener on the kitchen chair, "why it is that he is so obedient for his teachers in school and so ill-behaved at home." My father gets angry, too. "Why can't he get O in something that matters?" he asks.

"In my school," Polly said, "we get number marks, and we call it deportment, not conduct. I always get about fifty-five. Once I got fifty-nine. The teacher said I was doing better, but I wasn't good enough to pass."

"In my school we don't get marks in conduct at all," I said. "If we don't behave, we get invited to the headmistress's office and she sits us in a chair and talks about respecting our fellow human beings. I go to a private school."

"What's in your closet?" Polly asked Morton, getting up and opening its door. "Hey, what's all this? What's in all these bags?" She had discovered his collections.

"Trash," I said quickly. "That's where we keep the stuff we're going to throw out."

"They're my *things*," Morton told her. "They're my things that I find and I keep them."

Polly pulled a handful of bottle caps from one of the bags. "Oh, hey, look at these!" she cried. "Look at all of *these*!" and she let the little metal disks fall between her fingers like a bunch of loose beads. "This is the best stuff! Hey, watch what I can do!" She lifted up a blue bottle cap and held its sharp edges against her palm until it left a prickly ring on her skin. "Look! It makes designs! Here, Morton, give me your arm," and she pressed the cap up and down the arm where moments before the train had run. Little pleated circles like piecrusts sprang up along his skin, turning white and then red. "Isn't this great?"

"It's like flowers," Morton said, examining the rings on his arm.

"You have good stuff, Morton," Polly said. "You have really good stuff." She was back in the closet. "Hey, what's *this*?" She sank her hand into another of Morton's bags. "Oh, it's spoons! Look at all these spoons!" and she spilled them onto the floor. "Morton, you have the best stuff," she said again, lifting a plastic spoon and rubbing her tongue on the inside of its bowl. "What's in this bag here?"

"Special papers and things," Morton answered. "Candy papers and paper strings that I save. Nice red string from cigarette packs."

I didn't know Morton had collected so many cellophane strings. I didn't know there were so many strings to collect. There were more than Polly could hold in both hands. "Hey, we can make rain out of these," she said. "Watch this! Red rain!" She stood on Morton's bed and released a cellophane shower, slippery and red, onto the bedspread, the floor, the train, while Morton reached his hand out, and his tongue, too, to catch the drops before they fell. "Red rain!" he cried, flinging it all up into the air again. "Red rain!"

"Morton," I said. "You'd better clean that up before Mom comes home."

"I have the best stuff," Morton said, and he laughed out loud—too loud, which is how he always laughed whenever somebody said something nice about him. Aunt Sophia, usually.

"It's not *that* good," I told him, making my face stiff and blank, with no laugh in it at all, so he would know he wasn't as great as he thought.

"It's just junk," I said to Polly, "all that stuff. It's just old torn-up paper and a bunch of spoons that you get with your ice cream at the five-and-ten and that you're supposed to throw out. And anyway," I added, "we never finished doing our elbows. With my paint set. Let's have an elbow fight. We can make an elbow gang and give them names. This one will be Miranda," I said, crooking my arm at her face, "and this one is her twin sister Fanny." I don't know how I thought up those names. They just came to me, and I liked saying them in front of Morton, knowing he wouldn't understand. It was like telling a secret, not behind his back, but right out loud, and I felt him wondering, *What elbows? Who's Miranda?* "My sisters against your sisters," I went on. "Let's go back to my room and get the paints."

"No," Polly said. "I'm tired of that now." She picked up the coal car and spun its wheels hard against her palm. "Let's take this upstairs," she said. "To the roof." She spoke to Morton, not to me. "It will go on a trip up there," she went on. "To Africa."

"The roof!" I cried. "The *roof?* You're not allowed up there, Morton." He was already following her out of his room and into the hallway. "YOU'RE NOT ALLOWED UP THERE!" I shouted, but in another moment I heard the door of the apartment open and then close, and I realized all at once that Polly had not come to play with me at all. She had come to play with Morton, and she was going to be his best friend, not mine.

CHAPTER FIFTEEN

I picked up all the cellophane rain from the floor and
put it back in its bag. Then I nested the plastic spoons
together, bowl into bowl, and put them away, too. I
collected the bottle caps from the bed. I pressed one
against my own arm and watched as a little scalloped
pie shell turned red on my skin. I put all the train
things back, and after everything was cleaned up, I
walked around Morton's room, looking here and there,
and pausing finally in front of the envelope against the
clock. With a finger I traced the long curves of the M
and B of his name, and then I lifted it from the dresser
all at once and opened its flap.

When Morton started school last fall, my mother
bought a special arithmetic kit so she could help him
with math and he wouldn't be left back again. He was
left back in third grade and again in fifth, because he
was dumb, mostly in arithmetic. The new kit was part
of some special method that was supposed to be good

for dumb kids. Slow learners, they were called. Every evening, my mother would sit down with Morton at the kitchen table, and he would take all the things out of the box, one by one.

There were lots of things to take out. First came the instruction booklet that told you how to follow the special method. Then came a pack of flash cards held together with a rubber band, and then came a whole bunch of wooden sticks painted different colors. They were the best part—smooth and shiny, with nice straight edges so that they stood up tall, like a row of little men in suits of red and green and blue.

"Each red stick represents one hundred units," the booklet said, although that was not how you were supposed to explain it to the slow learner. "Each blue stick represents ten units, and each green stick represents one unit. Place ten green sticks in the student's left hand and one blue stick in his or her right hand. Then say, 'The green sticks are like pennies and the blue stick is like a dime. Ten green sticks are worth as much as one blue stick.' " On the next page the booklet showed how to combine the blue sticks and the green sticks to teach Number Concepts. "Reinforce this learning," it said, "with the accompanying flash cards."

"One blue stick and two green sticks make what number, Morton?" my mother would ask, and Morton would think awhile. "Twelve," he would say; he would get that right, because, although he's dumb, he's not that dumb. Then she would show him how to make more twelves out of the blue and green sticks, and when he had made four twelves, she would bring out the right flash card and show it to him: $4 \times 12 =$

"Four times twelve equals. Say that, Morton."

"Four times twelve equals."

"Now say, 'Four times twelve means four twelves.' "

"Four times twelve means four twelves." He would slip the rubber band from the flash cards over his fist and run it up and down his arm. Suddenly it would pop off and fly across the table. "Look at *that* one," he'd say, laughing his dumb laugh.

"*Listen* to me, Morton." My mother's voice would grow quieter instead of louder. Then she would recite the next phrase from the booklet. "Ask yourself: How many blue sticks in *one* twelve? How many green sticks? Ask yourself that, Morton."

"I just did."

"Out *loud*. Ask it so I can hear. Nice and loud."

"I forgot what to ask."

"How many blue sticks in *one* twelve? How many green sticks? Ask yourself that. Out loud."

"How many blue sticks in *one* twelve?" His voice would go way up on "one." "How many *green* sticks?"

"Now answer it. When you ask yourself a question,

Morton, the next thing to do is answer it. How many blue sticks in one twelve?"

"One."

"How many green sticks? *Count* them, don't play with them."

"Look," he'd say. "I made a blue M. For Morton."

After a while they'd have all the sticks arranged in the right number of rows, and she'd ask the last question: "Now. Four times twelve equals what?"

"Four twelves," he would answer.

"Morton! Four times twelve equals," and she would wait for him to answer something else dumb.

"Forty-eight."

"Be quiet, Mary Ella. I asked Morton."

"Forty-eight," he would say.

When half an hour was up, Morton would say, "Time's up," and he would put all the pieces of the kit back in the box, smoothing the rubber band over the flash cards and straightening the sticks into rows, so that everything looked nice and neat. I think he liked the arithmetic kit.

I slipped the report card out of its envelope and turned it over in my hand. Morton did get an *O* in conduct, and it hung like a little moon at the top of the page. He had a few S's too, in things like "Works Well With Others" and "Shows Respect for School

Property," but mostly he had N's for "Needs Improvement" and U's for "Unsatisfactory." At the bottom, next to where it said "Grade Placement for Next Year," his teacher had written the number seven, with one of those fancy lines through its stem, in black ink. Seven, not eight. For the third time since he began school, Morton was going to be left back. Retained, they called it.

When school started again in the fall, he and I would be in the same grade.

CHAPTER SIXTEEN

The little painted faces on my knuckles and knees had smeared by now into tattered streaks, and I went into the bathroom to wash them off. The colors floated away when I lowered my hands into the sink, and I watched them swirl around in the water—red, green, yellow, blue, stretching out like scarves in the wind. I stirred them around with my wrist, and all at once they were my orphan girls again—Vermilion, Emerald, Topaz, and Sapphire, dancing all together at their ball.

Round and round they went, their gowns flying smoothly from their throats and rustling as they brushed each other's hems. "Dance," I said into the sink. *"Dance!"* and they whirled around some more—faster and faster until they became no color at all, like pictures on a child's top: clowns and tigers and balloons that melt into a streak of gray when you push the plunger down. I pulled out the plug then and watched them rush away—all of them—down and away, down a darkened stair, laughing and whirling, to someplace I would never know. "Good-bye," I said to them, and then I washed my face and knees and wandered back into my room.

In an hour or so, my mother would come home, and she would ask where Morton was.

"He's with his new friend," I would tell her, but I wouldn't say where.

"New friend?" She would look pleased. "I didn't know Morton had a new friend. Who is he?"

"She. It's Polly."

"Polly! The new girl?" She would look disappointed now. "But I thought she was *your* friend."

"She was. Now she's Morton's." Would I be able to say that? Probably not.

Later, my mother would ask where Morton's report card was, and I would tell her it was on his dresser, leaning against the clock, but I wouldn't say I had already seen it myself. I would hold very still then and listen as she went into his room, and I would feel her eye running over the page until it came to the bottom where the seven stood, slanting like a garden hoe about to topple down. There would be a moment of quiet and then a sigh. A gasp, maybe. Then she would whisper something to her listener. "Stupid," or "impossible," she'd say, or "slow," the *s*'s hissing like water running into the sink, and although the words would be about Morton, I would feel as I do at Agnes Daly when the secrets in the hall are about me.

When I first began to hear my mother speak to her listener in the other room, I would go to the doorway and wait until she noticed me. "Tell me what you just said," I'd demanded one night, knowing she wouldn't. The girls in school never tell me their secrets either, even when the secrets are about somebody else. "Not meant for babies," they say, moving away and carrying their whispers with them. "Not for your ears," my mother had said then.

Now, though, I just stand still, wherever I am—in my room, in the hall, behind the bathroom door— and I listen all alone. I *make* myself listen, just as I make myself look when there's a dead bird in the street, or a squashed squirrel, so I can know how bad it is, all at once.

The little glass paint bottles still lay this way and that on the floor of my room, and I placed them one by one in a row along the desk. They were just a bunch of paints now—smeared-up paints with crazy names that didn't match. Eggshell was green; Ivory was blue.

Two colors only remained untouched: Crimson and Silver, and I twisted open their white metal caps. I lifted a sheet of paper from the floor and brushed a stripe across its face, thick and wet and red. It looked nice, like a lipstick streak, and I sat down at my desk to paint a picture, the first I'd ever painted out of school. It was the very same picture I made every night when I sat beside the rabbits in my Easter egg room: daisies in a bowl. This one was done on paper, though, not on little wooden eggs, and it wasn't quite as perfect. But it was lovely just the same—the bowl was almost round and the petals of the daisies were like silver insect wings, brittle and thin. I wrote "To Mother" across the top when I was through, but I was going to show it to my *real* mother this time, not a make-believe rabbit, and while she wouldn't say, "Oh, *exquisite*," she might say it was lovely. "Oh, lovely," and she would suddenly be very, very happy. So happy, in fact, that she wouldn't mind at all that Morton had a seven on the bottom of his report card instead of an eight, and that next fall he would be in the same grade as me, even though he was three years older.

CHAPTER SEVENTEEN

I put on some clean shorts after that and a nice white blouse—the one my mother liked best and that I wore last year when she took me—*just* me—to the ballet. Then I went up to the roof.

I'd never been up there before, and I put my foot over the doorsill cautiously, as though I were stepping into a cold lake. The floor was soft in the hot sun, and it gave way a little under my shoe. I couldn't see Polly and Morton anywhere, and I called out to them, but there was no answer.

Off in one corner, a line of clothes dried in the sun: shirts, fastened wrist to wrist, and underwear, too, hanging there for everyone to see. They rose, suddenly, all together, as though in alarm at the sound of my voice, and then fell. At the same moment a row of pigeons flew up from the branch of a TV antenna, their wings touching tip to tip, like the sleeves of the shirts, and then they, too, fell back and were still.

After that, nothing moved at all.

"Morton!" I called again. "Polly!"

It was scary up there, so far from where things were attached to the ground—far from the basements of buildings and the roots of trees—and I kept my eyes away from the sky. Stretching all around me was a field of tar, smooth and wide as a meadow, and as flat. It could have *been* a meadow, really, but one no longer green. Antennas stood along the walls like blackened trees, and chimney pipes, chipped and brittle, clustered like charred toadstools at their feet.

"Morton! Polly!" I moved away from the door and slid my feet along, as though I were nearing the edge of a cliff. *"Morton!"* And then I saw them on the other side of the roof, across the courtyard, heads down, walking slowly together. Like best friends.

When they got closer, I could see that Polly was pushing the coal car along the floor with her foot. "You're going to ruin that," I called out to her. "It's going to break if you do that." She picked the car up then and flew it around like a plane, making it dive and rise and do loops in the air. "And anyway, Morton, we're not supposed to be up here. We're not allowed."

"Why not?" Polly asked.

"Why do *you* think why not? Because we might fall off."

"How can you fall off? There's walls all around up

[*135*]

to your waist. You'd have to climb over them and jump, in order to fall off."

"Well, you could lean over or something and fall off that way. You could lose your balance."

"That's dumb. When you lean over a wall on the *ground* you don't lose your balance, do you? Hey, Morton, you want to make a shadow tower?"

"What?"

"A shadow tower. You want to make one? Look. See my hand's shadow? Now you put your hand's shadow on top of that. Then I'll put my other hand's shadow on, and then you put your other hand's shadow on, and then I'll put my head's shadow on, and we'll keep piling on a lot of shadows until we have a shadow tower."

Morton looked at his hands. "Which one?" he asked.

"This." She took his left hand and placed it above hers so that its shadow blotted out her own. "Now do this one."

"Don't do that, Morton," I said. She was going to play a trick on him after all. She would make him do crazy things with his arms and legs and then she would laugh when he fell down. People do things like that at Agnes Daly—to third graders, mostly. "Don't do it, Morton," I said. "It's a trick."

"It is," Polly said. "It's a shadow trick. It really works, too. You get a whole pile of shadows one on top of the other until there's a big tower, and then you jump in the middle of it like a haystack."

"That's dumb," I said. "That's the dumbest thing I ever heard." It *was* dumb. Not just silly dumb, but *dumb* dumb. Dumb like Morton, and suddenly I understood what was the matter with Polly: She was dumb. That was why she liked Morton. Because she was as dumb as he was. "Don't do it, Morton," I said. "You can't pile shadows on top of each other."

"You can so," Polly said. "We're doing it right now. Now do your head, Morton, on top of my head. How many shadows do you think it will take to make a tower three feet high?"

He looked up as he did when my mother asked a question from the arithmetic kit. "A hundred?" he guessed.

"Maybe. Look, let's make shadows from these shirts." She undid some of the clothespins on the line and held the drying wash up high so that it made a single dark map on the floor.

"You're not allowed to do that!" I yelled. "That's somebody else's clothes, and anyway, that's stupid, what you're doing. If you put one shadow on top of another it just makes one shadow." I was glad she wasn't my friend. She was even *dumber* than Morton.

"It does not. One shadow and one shadow makes two shadows, right? One and one is two, dummy."

"But not with *shadows*!" My throat hurt all the way up to my ears from yelling. "If you put one shadow on top of another it just *disappears*, sort of." Nobody had ever called me "dummy" before.

"Well, where does it go, then?" she asked, and I couldn't answer.

She took a piece of chalk from her pocket, and crouched down with it. "Look," she said, and I thought she was about to draw a diagram to explain how shadows added up, but she wasn't addressing me at all. "Look, Morton," she said, and she began tracing around the shadow of a chimney pipe, making the outline of a toadstool on the floor. She had forgotten about the shadow tower altogether. "Leave that there," she said. "Then, tomorrow morning when the shadow comes back, it will know where it's supposed to go."

Morton stared at the chalk outline. "Comes back?"

"Yeah. Shadows go away at night. They go up into the sky. That's what makes the dark. Didn't you know that?"

"Yes," he said.

"It does not," I shouted. "It does *not*! That's not what makes the dark. The sun goes down, that's what."

"Stand still, Morton," she said. "I'll do your shadow next." Morton stood with his hands and feet apart while Polly outlined his silhouette, moving the chalk up and down the tar to make arms and legs, and in and out to make fingers. "Don't move," she said, as the chalk traveled around his ear, his hair, his other ear, his neck, his shoulder, the little notch his sleeve made.

"There. Now take your shadow away." Morton stepped aside, pulling his shadow with him, and we all stared down at the empty outline sprawled flat on the roof. "Next time you come back," Polly told him, "your shadow will be waiting for you. It will know just where to go."

Morton grinned.

Suddenly, I wanted her to do my outline, too, even though she was dumb, or whatever she was, and I stood very straight, holding my shadow still on the tar, like a large paper doll colored black. *Do mine,* I whispered in my head. *Do mine, do mine, do mine,* but all she did was pick up the coal car and rub it across her palm. "You know what?" she said to Morton. "We could make real coal for this thing. You want to see?" She pulled another clothespin from the line and crouched with it over the floor. Overhead, two shirts swung by one arm apiece, like a pair of monkeys on a branch, and the underwear bounced. "Watch," she said, and I saw now that the tar floor really wasn't smooth at all, but puckered all over with fat black blisters. "Here's a nice juicy one." She plunged a leg of the clothespin into the tar's crust and a thick black liquid sprang out, making my mouth suddenly—surprisingly—water.

"Look," she said. "The roof is bleeding," and that made Morton laugh. Everything Polly said made him laugh. "That's a good one," he said. "The roof is bleeding."

"It is not," I told him. "That's just tar. Roofs don't bleed. Only people."

"Let's put a Band-Aid on it," Polly said, and she peeled off the strip on her forehead. I looked away at first, not wanting to see her scab, but there was nothing on her skin at all.

"What do you do that for?" I asked, suddenly curious. "Why do you wear a Band-Aid if you don't have a cut or anything?"

"I don't wear it," she answered. "I just keep it there in case I need it." She settled the gauze carefully on the broken bubble and pressed the ends out on the floor. "If I kept it in my pocket it would lose its stick."

"Hey, Mary Ella," Morton said, "the roof is bleeding," as though he had just thought of that himself, and with a finger he burst a whole cluster of bubbles, making them ooze. "The roof is bleeding," and he laughed his dumb laugh some more.

"Yeah," Polly said. "That's how they get coal. From roof blood," and she pulled the wet tar into a long string, sticky as licorice. "Watch." She molded a little ball between her palms and carefully dropped it into the hollow of the coal car. "Real coal. Let's make a whole lot."

They looked like two children in a sandbox, stooping side by side like that, messing with their hands. "Morton," I said, leaning against the wooden clothesline frame, "you'd better clean up your hands before you go downstairs. Mom will be mad if she sees you like that."

I thought about my mother suddenly. She'd be home by now, I realized, and she'd already have walked through all the rooms, wondering where we were, calling our names. She'd have walked into the kitchen, too, and seen my picture propped up on the table. I imagined her pausing at the kitchen door and drawing in her breath. "What's that?" she'd ask, hurrying in, and she'd lift it up carefully and carry it to the window. "Why, it's a watercolor," she'd finally whisper. *Watercolor*, she'd say, not picture. "By Mary Ella. What a lovely, lovely thing," and she'd hold it to the light. Then she'd stand it against the napkin holder and step back to see it better, the way people do in museums, putting her head to one side. "Look at how round the

bowl is," she'd say aloud, "and how red. Crimson."
She'd speak out loud, even though she was alone, and
not to her listener either—to *herself*.

"Mom will be mad," I said to Morton, and he stared
into his palms for a moment and then wiped them
across the front of his Mickey Mouse shirt. "Morton!"
I yelled.

"Oh, look," Polly said. "You drew a picture of a
fish. Wait, I'll give him an eye," and she stuck a little
dot of tar in the middle of Morton's stomach. He
laughed at that and then he said, "Mickey Mouse has
his own fish to eat now."

Polly added some more wads of tar to the pile in
the coal car, and then stood up. "Let's take it all for
a ride," she said.

"Let's take it to Africa," Morton said.

"Trains don't go to Africa," I told him.

"Yeah," Polly said. "Let's take it to Africa."

"And we can get on it," Morton said. "We can get
small."

"We can shrink ourselves. I know how, Morton.
You know why? Because I'm magic. I can shrink whatever I want. I can shrink all my clothes and everything,
and a whole bunch of food. Bananas and stuff. I can
shrink my grandma's icebox, too, to keep the food in.
I can even shrink my grandma, so she can come, too,

to wash our clothes and everything. I can shrink my chalk."

"And don't forget your toothbrush," Morton said. "So you can brush your teeth."

"Yeah. Except I don't have a toothbrush." She used the top of the roof wall for a track and ran the car along its edge, while Morton trailed behind, saying *"Rum-rum-rum."* Sometimes Polly said *"Rum-rum-rum,"* too. They went around all four sides of the building like that. I stood beside the clothesline and watched them go. "Morton!" I called out now and then, "don't get so close to the edge!" But he didn't answer, and after a while I stopped watching. Anyway, how could he fall over? Polly was right. The wall was too high.

Across the roof two pigeons sat, side by side on the branch of an antenna, not moving, and I squeezed my eyes open and shut at them, making them jump, making them double. A moment later, a third joined them, and they stood in a perfect row, like X's on a tic-tac-toe. They looked nice there, all three together, belonging to each other, and with a finger I drew a winning line through their bodies. *Stay,* I whispered to them. *Stay there,* and I held them down with my finger, but Polly suddenly shouted and they all flew away.

"Hey, Morton!" she called out. "Something's up ahead on the track!" They were on the right-hand side of the building now, away from the clothesline, away from me. The coal car was still between her fingers, zigzagging along the wall. "Look out! It's a cow or something! The car can't stop in time! It's going to hit the cow! It's going to derail! *Wham!*" and the little yellow car flew out of her hand and over the side of the roof.

CHAPTER EIGHTEEN

We all leaned over the wall, motionless as the three pigeons, and stared down at the next-door roof, one story below. Two, maybe. Even now I'm not sure.

The coal car had disappeared. "Where'd it go?" Polly asked.

"To Africa," Morton said. "That's Africa down there."

"It is not," I said. "That's a roof and your coal car is lost. It's gone. You're never going to get it back," and although I looked at him, it was Polly I really spoke to.

"Hey, look at all that stuff," she said. "There's lots of neat things on that roof."

There *were* lots of things down there: a long gray sock pressed flat into the floor, a scattering of clothes-pins, a comic book, a shoe. A shoe! How did a shoe get there? How did any of it? From some other roof or from the sky, because there was no door or stairway to the building underneath. Just a black glass skylight lying flat against the tar.

"*There* it is," Polly said suddenly, and she pointed to a spot in the corner where the tiny coal car lay, its wheels spinning into the sky like a turtle struggling to its feet.

"I see it," Morton said. "Look, Mary Ella. Over *there.*"

"I *know*, Morton. I have eyes, don't I?"

"It's upside down," he said. "Look, you can see its underneath," and he laughed, as though he were looking up somebody's dress.

"I told you," I said to Polly. "I told you it would fall over."

"No, you didn't," she answered. "You said Morton would fall over. You said the coal car would just break or something."

"I didn't say Morton would fall over. I said he *could.*"

"Well, he didn't. Just the coal car. And anyway, I can climb down and get it."

"No, you can't. It's too far down. And besides, there's no way to get back up."

"I know what," Morton said. "Use a rope."

"Very smart," I answered, sounding like Mrs. Pierce at Agnes Daly. "How's the rope going to hold her?"

"Not her," he said. "The coal car. The rope can get the coal car up."

"Hey, good idea," Polly said.

"Dumb," I said. "How's it going to stick?"

"Put tar on it," he said.

"That's the dumbest thing I ever heard."

"Let's do it," Polly said.

It took two clotheslines tied together to make a piece of rope long enough, and Polly had to take down all the rest of the wash to get at them. She scrubbed one end of the rope around in a broken tar blister until it was thick with goo, and then she lowered it slowly over the side.

"Hey," she called out to the coal car, "here's a nice fat worm." She twitched her wrist as though she were fishing. "Come and grab ahold!" The fuzzy tip bounced along the ground like a frightened insect, sticking nowhere. "Come *on!*" she yelled, and this time she swung the rope out as far as it would go, but it didn't hit the coal car at all.

"See?" I said. "It doesn't work. Nothing will. Your coal car is gone, Morton. You're never going to get it back. It's going to lie there forever. Even when you're all grown up, it's going to keep on lying there. Even when you're *dead*."

"No, it won't," he said. "I can jump down there and get it. You want to see? I'll put on my sneakers with all the rubber on the bottom. They're my climbing shoes. I can climb down things in those sneakers. And then I can climb up again. My sneakers stick to things."

"They do not," I said. "It's gone, Morton. Your coal car is *gone*."

"Look at the rope *now*!" Polly cried. She was still swishing it around, shaking it, making it shiver. "It's a skinny lady dancing on her toe. Look at her shimmy," and she rubbed it back and forth between her palms like a string of clay. "Now watch! She's doing that thing where you click your feet together in the air. You know? Like those people in the movies? What do you call that, Morton?"

"*Entrechat*," I told her, but she didn't look at me.

"Mom's going to be plenty mad," I said to Morton. Mrs. Pierce always says that: Plenty mad. "That train set cost a whole lot of money," I said. "You weren't supposed to take any of it out of the apartment. You weren't supposed to bring it up here. You're not supposed to be up here at all, in fact. Mom's not going to like it."

She *wasn't* going to like it. She was going to tell her listener a whole lot of things when she found out. She was going to say that Morton had no sense. She was going to say that he was stupid and disobedient and clumsy. She was going to say, "He would." That's what she always says, even when things happen to him that could happen to anyone else—to other kids in his class, to kids on the street, to me. "He would," she says when he gets sick or his jacket gets taken from his locker. "He would," when someone in the supermarket steps on his foot.

"He would," she said the day the toy sailboat was stolen, even though I was with him at the time and it was as much my fault as his. "He can't keep anything for more than five minutes," she said when we both stood before her in the kitchen, with nothing in our hands but a wet roll of string.

"It was more than five minutes," Morton corrected her. "It was a whole lot of hours."

It was, too. We had taken the boat to the park right after lunch that day and had sailed it in the lake all afternoon. It wasn't until the sky had turned the color of its own gray clouds and the tree reflections had darkened and grown heavy in the lake that the boat was carried off by some hands we never saw.

It had been a lovely boat, with a tiny steering wheel, a wire railing around its varnished deck, and a cloth sail that traveled up and down when you pulled a little string. It wasn't even ours. It had belonged to my father when he was little, and the only reason he let us have it was that I was the one who had asked, not Morton. "We'll just take it to the lake in the park," I had told him. "I won't let anything happen to it. I promise. I'll

[149]

take really good care of it," but it was Morton who was blamed when we came home with our arms hanging empty at our sides.

I had carried it through the streets myself that day, holding it down under my elbow as though it were a large bird, a fat goose or something, about to fly away. It was late October then, and the rowboats in the park were all chained together near the boathouse for the winter, so the sailboat had the lake all to itself. We tied it to a roll of kite string my father had given us, and we watched it wobble out to sea—what we *pretended* was sea—sometimes here, sometimes there. "All aboard!" Morton said when it reached the opposite shore, and at first I laughed, imagining a crowd of tiny foreigners climbing to its deck, but it's always a mistake to laugh at anything Morton says. He just says it over and over again after that, and that's what he did this time. "All aboard," he kept saying, even when the boat wasn't near the land at all. Finally I told him to stop. Once, it paused at a spread of lily pads and the tip of its sail leaned way over, pecking at the rim of a wide, flat leaf. "Look," Morton said. "It's getting a drink."

"No, it's not," I said.

Sometimes, when the wind fell, the boat would rest on the surface of the lake like a flower planted in water, while Morton tried to blow at it from the shore. Sometimes a sudden puff from somewhere would topple it over and it would wash, like a broken-winged gull, to our feet. Then we'd stand it up again and push it back out with long sticks, trying to steer it to the lily pads, to the other shore, to the big black island in the middle of the sea. But it followed private trails of its own. "Go!" I shouted at it. "Over *there!*" while it darted back and forth, sometimes too far, sometimes not far enough. "No, dummy! *There!*" I stretched my arms out wide to embrace the lake, to *tilt* it, like a puzzle where you roll tiny balls into the eyeholes of a face. "Go!" But the sailboat wandered where it pleased.

It must have been after five when the wind grew suddenly strong and the sailboat swept away like some wild living thing—a loon, maybe, or a swan—toward the crowd of wooden rowboats that huddled by the boathouse like a herd of sleeping cows. It bounced from boat to boat, and then rounded a bank where we couldn't see it at all.

"Last stop!" Morton called out. "Everybody off!" The roll of string spun out swiftly from his hand and then—surprisingly—the cardboard cone jerked away and hopped about on the ground. "Wo-wo-wo!" he cried, and I caught it under my heel, but the string continued to tug even after that, and a sudden sound of laughter came from somewhere far away.

The string grew quiet then and trailed loosely in the

water once again, gentle as seaweed. We watched it for a while, and then Morton began slowly to wrap it around the cone. "Come along, little boat," he said, pulling and winding, pulling and winding, but when he pulled the last of it from the water there was nothing tied to its end at all.

"He would," my mother said as we stood there in the kitchen, holding in our hands the coil of string, gray now and swollen with the wet of the lake. "He *would*," she told the light bulbs on the ceiling.

And now the coal car.

"Hey, Morton," Polly said, dancing the rope around some more on its fringed toe. "Look at her now. She's doing leaps. She can fly, even. Watch this!" The rope streamed out for a long moment and hung in the air like a bird, before falling back against the wall with a quiet slap. Morton laughed. "She bumped her head," he said. "The lady bumped her head on the wall."

"Yeah," Polly answered. "She bumped her head. Now she's going to jump way up in the air, about a hundred feet. Watch her go!"

Morton leaned over the wall and peered down. "That's good," he said, laughing again. "A jumping lady, like in the circus." He wasn't thinking about the coal car at all anymore.

"Hey, that's right, Morton. That's what she is—a circus acrobat. Now she's going to do her best trick of all. Ready?" Polly pulled the rope up and wound it around her hand to make a loose circle. Then she sailed it out like a Frisbee onto the roof below. "Look at her spin!" she cried.

"What did you do *that* for?" I shouted, looking down at the rope sprawled like a script S on the tar. "Why'd you do that? We could have used that rope. We could have gotten the coal car up with it, maybe. We could have figured something out. And anyway, it wasn't even yours. It belonged to the lady who hangs up the wash. That wasn't your rope!" I yelled.

"It's not a rope. It's an acrobat."

I leaned far over the wall and stared at the rope and the coal car. They would both lie there forever now, the coal car here, the rope there, belonging more to each other than they ever would to us. Forever. In the rain, in the snow, year after year. The make-believe coal would harden in the cold and ooze black blood in the sun. Ten years from now, twenty, when I was grown up, I'd come back up here, and the car would still be lying out of reach, its buttercup sides grown dark and its wheels turned to rust.

I decided to go downstairs after that, and I stepped over to the clothesline frame to fix myself up, so my mother would like the way I looked. I reached my hand up into my shorts to pull down my blouse, and I made comb teeth out of my fingers to smooth my hair. She wouldn't have to know where I'd been, or who with. "I was playing with a girl I know. Outside," I'd tell her, not lying. "How do you like my picture?" and she would look first at me, in my nice white blouse that she liked, and then at the picture still in her hand. "It's wonderful, Mary Ella," she'd say. "Just wonderful."

"*Rum-rum-rum,*" I heard all of a sudden, and I snapped my head around, thinking maybe Polly had gotten the coal car back after all, but she was only running her bunched-up fingers along the edge of the wall, making a toy car out of them. "*Rum-rum-rum,*" she said again, and then Morton made a toy car out of his fingers, too. "*Rum-rum-rum,*" they said together, and they crashed their hands one against the other. "*Wham!*"

Somehow, Morton had gotten tar on the back of his Mickey Mouse shirt, as well as on the front, and I knew all at once that my picture wouldn't make my mother happy after all. Nothing would. She'd be standing in the bathroom, not the kitchen, right now, and she wouldn't be exclaiming, "Oh, how lovely!" She'd be crying. The bathroom is where she always goes to cry; it's the only room with a door you can lock, and you can wash your face in the sink when you're through. I hear her in there sometimes, pretending to be coughing and letting the water run a lot. She'd be looking at her face in the mirror now, at her cheeks all splotched red and her eyes made narrow inside their lids. "Left back," she'd be saying to a towel, to the sink. "For the third *time*."

She'd be there still when I went downstairs, and when she finally came out later, she'd find Morton standing in the living room with tar all over his shirt. He wouldn't notice her face, and he wouldn't notice his report card, either. Instead, he'd tell her that the little coal car from his train set had fallen onto the next-door roof and you could see its underneath.

He and Polly were running their finger-cars over the side of the wall now, down toward the next-door roof, and Morton was leaning so far over I could no longer see his head. I didn't tell him to be careful, though. I didn't tell him anything at all. I just stood there for a long time, watching him, watching Polly; and then, suddenly, I did a dumb thing.

Even now I'm not sure why I did it. Maybe it was to make Polly like me more. Or my mother like me less. Maybe if my mother liked me less, she'd like Morton more. Maybe if Morton and I did the same dumb things, she'd like both of us the same. Anyway, instead of telling Morton not to lean over so far, instead of going downstairs, I crouched down and plunged all ten fingers into the black blisters on the roof floor. Then I dragged them across my chest, painting a blaze of stripes across my blouse—two rows of five stripes each, like staffs of music, on my nice white blouse, the one my mother liked best.

"Hey," I called out, standing up again. Polly and Morton raised their heads. "Look at me!"

Morton dropped his hand, spilling his make-believe car into the air, and stared at me. "Why'd you do that for?" he finally said. "Why'd you do that to your nice blouse?"

But Polly only laughed. "Hey, Mary Ella," she said. "Hey, M. E. That looks neat. It's like a picture. Of waves in the ocean or something. And that little spot there could be a boat."

"Mom will be mad," Morton said. "Your best blouse! Mom will be plenty mad." And he was right. My mother *was* going to be mad, plenty mad, and this time not at Morton, but at me.

CHAPTER NINETEEN

During the first few days after my mother found out that Morton was going to be left back, the house was very silent. No one spoke, and we passed one another on our way from room to room the way, in my school plays, people known as "passersby" crossed on the stage, pretending to be strangers.

It was a silence that comes over us whenever something terrible happens and Morton and I are not supposed to know. Up until then only two really terrible things had happened: My father's bookstore closed and he had to work for somebody else, and Aunt Sophia died. I was nine when she died, and my mother thought I was too young to hear news like that, so she didn't tell me, although I had been allowed to know all along that she was sick. "How's Aunt Sophia?" I used to ask during those long weeks, and my mother would sigh a lot and say, "Not well." But when she died, there were no words at all, and that was how I knew.

I had to pretend, though, not to know, so that when both my parents put on black clothes that hot summer morning and said they were going to a luncheon, I pretended to believe them. "Have a nice time," I called out, and I pretended even to myself that what they had said was true. I pictured them seated at a long table with a bunch of aunts and uncles, all eating their lunch—their luncheon—all wearing black. Aunt Sophia was there, too, at the head of the table, eating soup with a dainty spoon and talking first to the guest on her right and then to the one on her left, and finally to my mother and father down the table.

For a week after that, for two weeks, the house stayed silent, and once, to show my mother that I hadn't guessed her secret, I asked again, "How's Aunt Sophia?" But this time she answered, "Oh, she's better. She's all better," and that was the last time we ever mentioned Aunt Sophia's name. I never even got to cry for her, because she wasn't supposed to be dead, but I wish I could have, because she was my favorite aunt.

Now the house was silent again, and this time, too, I tried to let my mother think I didn't know her secret. "When Morton goes to eighth grade," I said one day, "he's going to have Miss Pines, who everybody on the block hates," and she answered, "We'll see." When would she tell me? When would I be allowed to know?

I never saw the report card again, and I don't know where it is even now. Hidden in a drawer somewhere, probably, or thrown out. It had stayed propped up against the clock on Morton's dresser all that afternoon and all that night, too, because, as things turned out, my mother never got to see it that day at all. She didn't even discover it herself; Morton showed it to her at breakfast the next morning.

Nothing, in fact, turned out as I expected it to that day. My mother didn't learn about the lost coal car until weeks later, and she didn't even see the tar on my blouse. She wasn't crying in the bathroom when I went downstairs, and she wasn't staring at my picture of daisies in a bowl. She wasn't even there. She was late coming home, and my painting still stood where I had left it on the table.

I picked it up and looked it over. It really wasn't so great. Pictures never are the second time you look at them, and anyway I didn't want her to see it at all by then. So I tore it up. I made a long crooked rip through the middle of the page, cracking the crimson bowl and splintering the daisies with their slender silver wings. Then I put the pieces in the wastebasket and sat down in the living room where my mother would see me first thing when she came home, with my ears sticking out of my hair and the black tar streaked across my blouse like tire tracks on snow.

Where she'd see that *I* did dumb things, too. Not just Morton.

But when she finally came home, she didn't look at me at all. "Where's Morton?" she demanded, and I suddenly realized it had grown late and Morton and Polly hadn't come back downstairs. "Why didn't he meet me at the barber's?" she went on. "Where *were* you? Why didn't anybody answer the phone?"

"He was supposed to meet you at the barber's?"

"You knew that, Mary Ella. Where *is* he?" She walked past the couch and into his room.

"He's not there," I said, following her. "He's outside. Playing with Polly." I didn't say where.

"Who's Polly?"

"The new girl. I told you about her. She lives on Preston Street with her grandmother. She's Morton's friend," I added, wanting her to know that, to know that Morton had found a friend, although he had lost his train car and had tar all over his clothes and was being left back in school for the third time.

"Where are they? I didn't see them on the street."

"They're around," I said. "I'll go find them," and I walked right past her with my ruined blouse.

*   *   *

"Morton?" I called from the doorway of the roof. "Mom wants you. You were supposed to have a haircut." Everything seemed different up there now. The air was strangely cool and very still. Nothing moved. The wash was all taken down and the pigeons, too, were gone, as though, like the laundry, they'd been carefully unpegged and folded flat and smooth into a drawer. Only the chalk outline of Morton's body seemed the same, sprawled like a clothesline on the floor. If I waited long enough, I wondered, would his shadow creep back in, as Polly had said, and fill up all the space?

"Polly?" I called.

Nobody answered.

"Morton!" I raised my voice this time. "It's getting late!" and my words floated like bubbles through the air. "Polly!" Where were they, anyway? My eyes wandered over to the wall on my left, and suddenly I felt a shiver dart through my body. A *hot* shiver. The coal car lay on the other side of that wall, one story below—two, maybe; anyway, it was far—on a roof that had no door. I could go over and look if I wanted, but I didn't move.

"There's walls all around up to your waist," Polly had said. "You'd have to climb over and jump, in order to fall." Morton's waist, too? I tried to measure from where I stood. Anyway, when you lean over a wall on the *ground* you don't fall off, so why should you fall off up here? Polly had said that, too, but what if they didn't fall by mistake? What if they had tried to *climb* down there? To Africa, where Polly had wanted to go, and Morton, too.

"I can climb down there in my climbing shoes," Morton had said, and then what had *I* said? Had I told him no, he couldn't? I tried to remember. Had I told him no, he couldn't in his *sneakers*, but he could in his regular shoes? I shook my head to rattle the thought away.

"MORTON!" I shouted, and his name broke against a chimney pipe, making a small ring.

It was a long time before I stepped over the sill and onto the tar, and when I finally did, it wasn't to go over to the wall. Instead, I walked around the opening of the courtyard and over to the front of the building. *They're probably down on the street*, I thought. *Playing or something*, and I leaned way over to look.

Right down below me, in a straight line under my nose, stretched the top of the awning, looking strange from so far up—flat as a strip of tape and no wider than the space between two fingers.

People were down there on the sidewalk: Franklin, Ina, Henry, Charles. I knew them from the tops of their heads. They moved around as fish do in a pool, slipping back and forth—here, there, in, out—never touching. Polly and Morton could be down there, too, I thought. They could be just inside the doorway, out of sight, like minnows in the shadow of a rock. With the drop of a pebble I could startle them into view.

I lifted a chip of broken chimney and held it out high above the canvas. In a moment—longer than I thought—I heard its tiny plop, and I caught my breath, watching, waiting for two shapes to dart into the sun, but nothing stirred. I finally turned back and walked around the roof, high above the courtyard, until I came to the wall where the coal car lay.

I shut my eyes when I got up close. I kept them shut until my toes bumped against the wall, and then I lifted them little by little, as I would lift a page in a scary book.

Morton's coal car lay quietly on its back in the puddle of its own shadow, looking small, and Polly and Morton were nowhere to be seen.

CHAPTER TWENTY

"They're missing," I said, liking the alarm of the words. "They were up on the roof," I explained, "and now they're gone." I looked from Ina to Deirdre to Justine.

"Polly and *Morton?*" Ina asked. "Polly's playing with *Morton?*"

"How come she's doing that?" Deirdre asked.

"I don't know," I answered. "He has this train she likes."

"Weird. What's that stuff on your blouse?"

"It's tar," I told her. "From the roof."

"From the roof? What were you doing on the roof?"

"Nothing much. Playing. With Morton and Polly. She's his friend." And then, all of a sudden, I remembered something Polly had said up on the roof. I didn't *remember* it, exactly; I *noticed* it, for the first time. "Hey, Mary Ella," she had said, and she had laughed as I showed her the tar on my blouse. "Hey, M. E.

That looks neat." For the first time ever, somebody had called me M. E., and I turned to Ina and Justine and Deirdre and gave them my biggest smile. "She's my friend, too," I told them.

"You were up on the *roof*?"

"Yeah. It's nice up there. There are pigeons and things and these bubbles you can break to make the roof bleed."

They all looked at me after I said that, and then Ina asked, "Does your mother know?"

"No. But anyway, she wouldn't care. She lets me do whatever I want." That's not what I tell my friends at Agnes Daly. I tell them my mother doesn't let me do anything at all, so they'll think I'm rich, like them. Wanda's mother doesn't even let her walk to school by herself, even though she lives closer than I do, and Peggy's mother makes her wear long underpants until the end of April, so her legs will keep warm. You can see them when she walks up the stairs.

"So if you were up there with them, how come you don't know where they are?" Justine asked.

"Because they stayed up there some more after I went home."

"Maybe they fell." It was Ina who said that.

"How could they fall?" I said. "The walls are up to your waist all around. People don't fall over walls like

[*165*]

that when they're on the ground, do they? And any-way, I looked." Except not everywhere, I suddenly remembered. Not in the courtyard.

Pretty soon everyone on the block was looking for Polly and Morton, and by then I had begun to hope that something terrible really had happened to them, so that Deirdre and everybody wouldn't feel cheated, going to all that trouble for nothing. We really didn't know where to look, and so we looked in a whole lot of dumb places—under cars, in the sewer, in trash cans, behind the hedge—as though it were a stray jack ball we were tracking, and not two people with legs that could take them far away.

"Maybe they were kidnapped," someone said.

"Them? Who would want to kidnap *them?*"

"Maybe someone stole them, to sell somewhere."

"Maybe they fell," Ina said again. "Maybe they're lying in some alley somewhere. All broken up."

"I told you," I repeated. "You can't fall. There's walls all around."

"So? Maybe they were walking on top of the walls. Polly does things like that."

"Yeah," Henry said. "She's crazy. She does crazy things. Yesterday she took this piece of chalk she al-ways has and she drew a line around the whole block—one long line on all the buildings and on the fences and on the bushes even, and when she got back to where she started she drew a bow, like she was tying up a present or something in a ribbon."

"She eats leaves, too. Every day she eats leaves from those bushes."

"She wrote a note on a piece of paper and mailed it in the sewer. She said she knows somebody who lives down there."

"She hung on the back of a bus and rode it for a whole block. I saw her."

"Maybe that's where they are now. On the back of a bus."

"Maybe they're running away. Maybe they're running away to where she comes from."

"Where does she come from?"

"I don't know. Someplace far away. She talks funny."

"She talks crazy."

"She *is* crazy."

"I bet they fell off the roof."

Maybe they were right: Polly was crazy. Not dumb, *crazy*. Maybe that was why she liked Morton. Somebody who ate leaves and mailed things in the sewer would be crazy enough to like Morton. Maybe that was why she liked me, too—because I put tar on my blouse and she thought it was nice.

And then all of a sudden there she was, walking up the street, chewing on a piece of bread. Alone.

"Hey, Polly!" someone shouted. "How did you get down?"

"What?"

"Where's Morton?"

"Who? Oh. I don't know. Still at the movies, probably," she answered through a wet crust. "Hey, M. E.," she said to me. "You want to play jungle?"

"At the movies!" I stared at her. "Morton's at the movies? What's he doing there?" Morton never goes to the movies. I don't go much, either. My parents think movies are bad for your eyes, and anyway, they never want to spend the money.

"Where'd he get the money?" I asked.

She pulled the piece of bread out of her mouth and I saw that it wasn't really bread at all. It was a thin white sock bunched up in a ball. "What money?"

"To get in," I said. "To the movies." But by then I realized that they had gone in without paying at all. "How come he's still there and you're not?" I asked.

"I'd already seen that movie. Do you want to play jungle, M. E.? We can be apes."

"No." I wanted to go upstairs. I wanted to tell my mother that Morton had done a wonderful thing. I wanted to tell her that he had gone to the movies with a friend, without telling anyone where they were going, when he was supposed to meet my mother at the barber's, and that they had sneaked in without paying. I wanted to tell her that Morton, for once, had done something disobedient—really disobedient, like other boys—and not just dumb.

"Did you find him?" she asked when I walked through the door.

"Yes," I said, "and don't be mad." That's what Ezra's sister says to *her* mother when she explains where Ezra is or what he's done, but what I really wanted to say was, "Be mad. Not mad the way you usually are, whispering to your listener in the kitchen or telling about what any other mother would do, but really mad. Like any other mother. Like Ezra's mother, who shouts a lot and says that Ezra has the devil inside him."

"He went to the movies," I said. "He and Polly went to the movies and they sneaked in without paying. Like Ezra. Ezra does that all the time. And Franklin, too, sometimes." Then I stood back and waited for her to be secretly glad that at last Morton had done something like other boys on the block.

"Good," she said, and for a minute I thought she *was* glad. "Good. Wonderful," and then I knew she wasn't. "When he was supposed to meet me at the barber's. When he could have been outside. A beautiful day like this and he spends it at the movies. Ruining his eyes. He has as much sense as a toad," she said to the kitchen clock.

A toad? Is that what she had said? A *toad*? I'd never heard her say that before. As much sense as a toad, and suddenly I thought of Morton crouched on a seat at the movies, all wet and shriveled and the color of mud, blinking at the screen with eyes that bulged from each side of his head—a toad—and something inside me wanted to cry. Instead, though, I thought of some-thing.

"Look what I did to my blouse," I said. "I got tar on it. I was playing up on the roof, and I got this tar all over my best blouse, and I don't think it will wash out ever."

JULY

CHAPTER TWENTY-ONE

The strange thing is that, except for the beginning, when Morton got left back, and the end, when everything went wrong, this was the best summer I'd ever had.

It used to be that all my summers were the same. As soon as my parents left for work and Morton left for summer school, I'd go into my room and look for something to do. First, maybe, I'd try to read some hard book that I'd gotten out of the library to make the librarian think I was smart, and then I'd play with my orphan girls for a while. Or I'd write a letter to Wanda at camp and tell her what a wonderful time I was having. Then I'd put my face up close to the mirror and practise different smiles. Sometimes I'd take all the socks out of my drawer and make a parade, but mostly I did nothing. I'd just stay in the house all day until my mother came home from her job and told me it was a crime to be indoors on such a beautiful day.

"A crime," she would say.

"But there's nothing to do outside."

"How can there be nothing to do?" and she would list all the things she would do if she were young and had no responsibilities. "I'd take a good long walk somewhere," she'd say, putting out her chest as though she really *were* taking a walk. "I'd take a book to the park and read it on a bench. I'd get together with a whole group of friends and plan a picnic." When she was my age she always had a whole group of friends who did things together. Outdoors. "I'd organize a game."

"Nobody is around," I would tell her. "Everyone from school is at camp, and everyone on the block is doing something." Playing with each other, was what.

"Why don't you go downstairs and call for someone?" she would say, not listening.

Call for. That's what her friends did all the time when they were young. They would call for each other, ringing each other's doorbells, and then they'd go outside together and organize nice games.

Finally she'd say what I waited for her to say every day and hated to hear: "Why don't you call for Audrey?" Audrey was the daughter of one of her friends. She lived six blocks away and was almost three years older than I was. "She'd be glad to have someone to play with, Mary Ella."

"She's too old," I'd tell her.

"But you're used to older girls. You have loads of friends in school and they're all older than you."

"But Audrey's in high school, practically."

"She'll have a lot to teach you, then. Call for her, Mary Ella. She's a lovely girl."

She *was* a lovely girl—smart in school, pretty. Besides that, she had good manners. She said, "How are you, Mrs. Briggs?" when she passed my mother on the sidewalk, and she helped people pull their shopping carts home. When I see people's mothers coming up the street I bend down to tie my shoe.

"Call for her, Mary Ella," my mother always said, and one day I did.

I stood in front of her apartment door for about ten minutes before I managed to ring the bell, and it took her a long time, too, to answer it. She looked a little rumpled when she finally appeared, and at first she didn't know who I was.

"Do you want to go for a good long walk somewhere?" I asked, putting out my chest.

She squinted at my face in the dark hallway. "What?"

"Do you want to take a walk? To the park or something? We could take a picnic along. Or we could play a game."

"Oh, it's Mary Ella. I'm sorry, Mary Ella. I'm busy

[*175*]

now." And then I saw she already had a friend with her. A boy.

"She already was playing with somebody else," I told my mother when I returned home.

"Well, why didn't you ask them *both* to go with you? They would have been glad to get out in the fresh air on such a nice day."

This summer, though, everything was different. Suddenly, for the first time ever, I had a best friend and we played together every day. Sometimes we went to her grandmother's apartment and sometimes we came to mine. Sometimes we went to the park, and sometimes, on hot mornings, we just sat on the sidewalk in front of her building, letting its shadow chill the backs of our legs. All morning long we would sit there, not doing anything, sliding slowly back along the shadow as it moved from curb to front step, until it disappeared entirely, like a letter slipped under a door, and we knew it was time for lunch.

Sometimes we didn't bother with lunch at all, and after a while we didn't bother to wash either, even before dinner, even after we'd floated privet leaves in mud for an hour.

It was nice, being dirty. I liked rubbing the sweat on the inside crease of my arm to make black crumbs, and I liked scraping at the dark stripes, thick as crayon wax, that filled the spaces under my fingernails. I liked the new things I could do with my hair, now that it was sticky—tie it into little knots that stayed for hours and paste it against my forehead in flat rings. I liked letting my nose run and, like Morton, licking off my wet upper lip with my tongue. Also, there was a heavy smell, like a warm cage, under my arms, and I liked that, too.

It was nice doing a lot of things Polly and I did together. Wherever we went she took her chalk with her and marked up places where we'd been. Sometimes she just ran it along the sides of a building as we walked, so that a thin strand of white uncurled behind her like a trail of spider silk. Sometimes she paused and drew a picture on the sidewalk—of a face, a cat, a bug. Or she'd write her name, outlining the letters so she could color them in, and giving them a bar to stand on when she was through.

Sometimes she would add LOVES POLLY to a name already written on a wall: BOB LOVES POLLY, she would make it say, or POLLY LOVES BOB. Even when somebody already loved someone else, she'd add her name: STEWART LOVES JILL AND POLLY it says—still, to this day—on the inside of a tunnel in the park.

A week after Morton's school closed, it opened all over again, for summer-school kids. Morton had to get up early every day, just as he did the rest of the year, and walk the same seven blocks, carrying the same lunch and the same books to the same dark building behind the same wire fence. "He mustn't be allowed to neglect his *skills*," the principal told my mother, as she tells her every summer, even though this time he wasn't going to be promoted and summer school wouldn't do him any good. Every summer it's the same. He spends the mornings doing arithmetic and reading, so he won't neglect his skills, and the afternoons doing Creative Recreation, which means making lanyards out of plastic strings and bug cages out of Popsicle sticks.

This summer, though, was different for Morton, too. For the first time ever, instead of spending the after-noons alone in his room when he came home, he'd go to Polly's house or she'd come to ours, and then I'd stay alone in my room, because I wasn't the only best friend Polly had. Morton was her best friend, too, and she played with us one at a time.

"Where's Morton?" my mother asked one day when she found me alone.

"Playing."

"Playing where?"

"At his friend's."

"What friend's?"

"Polly's."

"Polly's! I thought Polly was your friend."

"She is. She's both of ours."

My mother was silent for a while. "What kind of girl is that who plays with you and with Morton, too?" she asked.

"I don't know," I answered. "She likes us both. And anyway, we're not that different, Morton and me."

And by that time we weren't.

CHAPTER TWENTY-TWO

"Look at the twins," I heard someone say, and I looked up to see.

It was a Sunday and we were all in the park together—Morton, my mother, my father, and me. I was walking side by side with Morton, matching my step to his, sliding my feet the way he does, tripping sometimes and moving so slowly that my mother and father, far behind us to begin with, soon caught up, and my mother stepped on the back of my shoe.

"Walk *ahead*," she said. "Move faster, Morton."

"Come on, Mary Ella," Morton said. "Don't walk like that," and for a while we quickened our pace.

It was the hottest day of the summer so far. The sky was the color it gets on days like that—the color of steam—and imaginary puddles kept springing up in the roadway far ahead—wide, rippling pools of black that flattened out to nothing when we got up close. I kept my head down, like Morton's, and looked at

things along the road: a spilling of Crackerjacks, sometimes a whole boxful, here and there, and Styrofoam
cups stained brown along the rim. Morton picked up
a cup and dropped cellophane strings into it for his
collection, and I dropped things into a cup, too—
matchbooks, because by then I had started a collection
of my own.

"Look, Mary Ella," he said, tightening a cellophane
string around his fingertip. "My finger has a sunburn."
I laced a string around my own finger and watched the
tip grow red, liking the ache it sent into my hand.

"Look at the twins," someone said from a bench,
and I lifted my head to see.

I liked looking at twins. I liked to see two people
exactly alike, with the same hair and the same clothes
and the same face. The same walk, and maybe even
the same talk, too—the same words coming out of
both mouths at the same time.

I always used to wish *I* could be twins.

"Let's pretend we're twins," I said to Wanda one
day last year. "Let's go to the park and fool people."

"Twins?" she asked, staring at me. "How can we do
that?"

"We'll dress alike and make ourselves look alike and
everything. You want to?"

"Okay. Who'll be the real one and who'll be the
twin?"

"What?"

"Which do you want, you be my twin or me be yours?"

"I don't care," I answered, although I did care. *I* wanted to be the real one, the one with the double, and I wanted her to copy my clothes and my face and make her hair like mine, with the red highlights and all. "Which do you?"

She looked me over for a long moment, examining my T-shirt, which that day had a little hole just under the collar, and my face, which was all red and streaked from a cold. "You be mine," she said. "We can wear my camp clothes, which are all alike, and you can wet your hair to make it straight."

Wanda's hair is light and smooth, and when she shakes her head it moves all in one piece, like the fringe on a curtain. Now and then she takes a strand between two fingers and slides it behind her ear, and I tried that now, with a piece of my wet hair. It felt lovely, with the air sudden and cool against my ear, and I could see why she wanted me to be her twin and not the other way around.

We gave ourselves twin names—Jeanie and Janie— and we went to the park, wearing our matching shorts and shirts and keeping our feet in perfect step.

"This is nice," Wanda said, "being twins. If my sister and me were twins we could wear the same clothes all the time and do everything together and be in the same class. That would be neat."

"Yeah," I said.

"And then my mother wouldn't like her best anymore. She'd like us both the same."

We stayed in the park all day, walking along the paths, waiting for someone to notice. When no one did, we called each other "Twin." "Oh, look, Twin," I shouted, pointing into a tree, "I see a sparrow," and she shouted back, "Oh, yes, Twin. I see it, too."

"Come *on*, Mary Ella," Morton said. "Don't do that."

"Don't do what?"

"What you're doing. Walking funny and everything."

"How funny?"

"*You* know. With your head like that and all. Walk normal, like you always do," and I realized all at once that the twins those people saw were really Morton and me.

Two dumb twins. Walking alike, looking alike, *being* alike. Picking stuff up off the ground alike and wearing clothes alike, too; we both had on our shirts with the tar streaks, and our socks had slid into our shoes.

Someone even liked us both the same.

CHAPTER TWENTY-THREE

"I could tell you belonged to Morton the minute you walked through that door." Polly's grandmother was wearing an apron that reached to the floor, and she looked over at me from the kitchen sink. "You have the same walk, the same look in the eye. You hold your head the same, too," she said, putting her chin down to her chest, copying Morton, copying me. "Odd," she said.

I was visiting Polly's apartment for the first time, in the beginning of July, and I stood at the kitchen door a long time, looking in. *Squinting* in, really, because although the morning sun shone heavily on the sidewalk outside, the light that came through the window was an evening light, thin and gray, and it took me a while to see.

There were things in there that nobody ever puts into a kitchen: a dresser with a mirror and the kind of chair that belongs in a living room—big and stuffed and covered in something green. A pillow of spotted fur lay in its corner. Everything looked old.

Polly's grandmother looked old, too. Her face was like the charcoal drawings we do in art class, where we sketch in lots of lines, sharp and thin, and then rub them to a shadow with the edges of our hands. Her hair was like her face—all lines and shadows— but her hands were strangely pink and shiny bright. Big pink hands she had, clinging to her hips and dripping suds, and then I saw that she was wearing rubber gloves.

"Odd," she said again. "So very odd," and I could tell that *she* belonged to *Polly*. Not from the way she walked or held her head, but from the way she talked. "Suh very odd." She turned back to the sink, and I noticed then that she was wearing Polly's skirt—the one with the stripes that Polly had worn the day we met, and the shirt was Polly's, too. How come Polly let her grandma wear her clothes? I wondered.

She lifted something slowly from the sink—something long and fat—and grasped it at its center, wringing hard. Tighter and tighter she twisted until it kinked into a loop, and then, with a snap that made me jump, she shook it loose. It was another one of Polly's shirts, and her grandmother hung it on a rack with wooden arms. "There now," she said, buttoning the collar and smoothing out the sleeves. "All dressed," and she stepped back to admire the rack that stood now like a scarecrow in the middle of the floor.

"You even dress the same," she said, looking me over some more, and I glanced at my clothes. I had put on one of Morton's Mickey Mouse shirts that morning, a gray one with black borders at the sleeves and collar. "How come you're wearing my shirt?" he had asked me. "Mom, Mary Ella's wearing my shirt." He wasn't angry; he was disappointed. "Why don't you wear something nice?" he had asked.

"I always wear my brother's clothes," I told Polly's grandmother, liking the way that sounded. The girls in Agnes Daly wear their brothers' clothes, too: big gray sweatshirts with the name of some high school printed on their fronts, and, in the winter, long striped scarves, maroon and gold. Not Mickey Mouse shirts.

"Even down to your shoes," Polly's grandmother added, although my sneakers were my own. They were just untied.

How did she know, I wondered then, what Morton's shoes were like? How many times had he been here, anyway? "What do you do here," I asked Polly, "when Morton comes?"

"Nothing much. Play games. Mess around."

Still, I wondered. The only time anybody had ever invited Morton to their house, it was to play a trick on him.

"Hey, Morton," Henry had once said. "Come to my house tomorrow at three o'clock. I'm having a party."

"Where do you live?" Morton had asked.

"Down there," and he laughed as he pointed into the stairway that led to a cellar. Nobody went into the cellar. Rats lived down there and old men, too, sometimes. Justine had seen someone in a torn shirt come up the steps one day and blink at her in the glare. And once, in its doorway, we had found a single shoe. "Where'd this come from?" Ina asked, picking it up, turning it over, swinging it by its lace. She held it to her ear for a moment, as though, like a seashell, it held an echo of where it had been, but then Franklin said, "It's the old man's," and she dropped it on the stairs while we all ran away.

Morton didn't try to go to Henry's house, but he did go to Justine's once when she and Ina and Ezra invited him. I never found out what had happened, because he never told, and they didn't tell either, but one time I heard Ina say, "Remember when Morton came to Justine's?" and everybody laughed.

"*How* mess around?" I asked Polly.

"I don't know," she answered. "We just do stuff."

Suddenly the fur pillow on the chair began to move in its corner, and I jumped back.

"Here, kitty, kitty," Polly said, and the pillow jumped

down to the floor. "Come here," she said to it, and she stooped down to drag a finger through its hair.

"Is that a cat?" I asked. "I mean, is that yours?" I moved back some more.

"Yeah. She has fleas. You want to see? I can make them come out. Hey, flea!" she shouted, and she snapped her fingers. "Come make friends with M. E. Sit still, kitty, so the flea can shake hands. SIT!" But the cat walked out of the room.

"What's its name?" I asked, watching it go.

"Kitty. I already said that."

"No, I mean its real name."

She stared at me. *"Kitty."*

"Kitty? That's all you call it?"

"What's wrong with that?"

"I don't know. That's what people call cats that don't have a real name."

"They do so have a real name," Polly's grandmother said from the sink. "It's Katherine. Kitty is what you call *anyone* who's named Katherine. It's a nickname. Didn't you ever know that?" She turned around to stare at me. *"Didn't* you?" she repeated, when I didn't answer.

"No. I mean I didn't know it about cats."

"Well, you do now." She turned back to the sink.

"Let's play, M. E.," Polly said, and she led me through the kitchen into the living room.

The living room was dark, too, darker even than the kitchen. Polly pulled at a hanging string and a little cluster of bulbs lit up on the ceiling. There wasn't much to see: a table with a radio on it, a picture of a pyramid and a camel taped to the wall, a couple of wooden chairs. But there were two sofas instead of one, and the room looked crowded.

"You want to watch bugs?" Polly asked.

"Bugs? Fleas, you mean, from your cat?"

"No, a different kind. These live on the ceiling."

I looked up. "You have bugs on the ceiling?"

"Yeah. They come out after the light goes on. Lie down and we can watch them. They do tricks and everything, like at the circus."

Polly lay down on the wooden floor, and after a while I lay down, too. I didn't see any bugs at all— just little spider strings hanging like stray hairs on a chin or joining one light bulb to another.

"Are they spiders," I asked, "the bugs?"

"No. They're bugs. They'll come out in about a minute, first one and then the other. They go over to each other like they're about to kiss, but then they change their minds and they move away."

We lay there for a long time staring at the ceiling and at the ring of lights, but no bugs came. When I closed my eyes, a circle of blue disks clung to my lids,

[189]

and I watched them brighten and fade. Maybe that's what Polly thought were bugs. Eye spots.

I didn't care, though. It was nice lying there, with a real friend, and I tried to think of something to say to her. What? Mostly, at Agnes Daly, friends say something like, "You want to trade sweatshirts for keeps?" and they go into the bathroom and come out wearing each other's clothes. Or they trade spit. "Let's be spit sisters," they say, and they spit into their own hands and rub each other's palms. Sometimes they say things about someone they hate. Me, usually. Standing by the lockers or against the washroom door, I will catch a sudden whisper and I'll stop to tie my shoe or wipe my nose. Mostly, all I hear is lots of *She*'s. *She, she, she*, rustling like two fingers at my ear. But now and then my name will come: Mary Ella, I will hear, each syllable floating down the hall like a balloon and exploding at my shoulder with a pop.

What could I say to Polly?

And then I thought of something.

"Polly," I said, "do you think it can happen"—and I turned my eyes from the ceiling so I could look into her face—"that games come true?"

"What?"

"Not the Monopoly kind of game. The other kind, where you play that something happens. Something bad. Do you think that?"

"Games come true? Like what?"

"Like broken leg or scarlet fever? Make-believe games? Somebody told me that once. If you play you're poor you get poor, and if you play that somebody dies they really will. Do you think that—that games come true?"

"I don't know. Anyway, so what if they do? What's so terrible about that?"

"Well, what if you get to be poor or somebody dies or something or you break a leg, just because you played it once?"

Suddenly, that sounded like a dumb thing to believe, but I believed it anyway. Lots of times I believe things even though I know they're not true. "If you touch stone, you turn to stone," Wanda used to say, and even now, sometimes, I keep my hands against my side when I walk beside a building made of stone instead of brick.

"So?" Polly said. "I'm poor. And somebody died. The only thing, I didn't break a leg. But it wouldn't be so bad if I did. I'd get out of helping my grandmother in the house and going to the store for her all the time."

I was silent for a long while after that, and finally I said, "Somebody died?"

"Yeah. Two people. First my other grandmother and then my father. That's why I'm here. Because my mother couldn't afford to keep me and my sister both. So she sent me up here and she kept my sister Irene, and anyway, she likes my sister best."

She didn't seem to mind very much that her mother liked her sister best. She didn't whine about it the way everybody else I know does. "She likes your sister best?" I asked.

"Yeah. My father did too," and then I said something I'd tried out before only in my head. "Me too," I said. "My parents like my brother best." The words made a little echo in my ear. It was a nice thing to say to a friend, even though it wasn't true.

"Probably because he's nicer," Polly said, "like with my sister."

"Yeah," I answered. "Probably," but I thought about that. Morton was nicer? He was? I had always thought *I* was nicer. I do lots of nice things for people. I let people get in front of me in the supermarket line if they have only one thing to buy, and once, in the park, I read the newspaper to an old lady who couldn't see. Also, I helped a little kid find her mother once, and in school sometimes I let people copy my answers on spelling tests. Morton never does things like that.

But maybe Polly didn't mean that kind of nice. Maybe she meant that Morton never argued back.

CHAPTER TWENTY-FOUR

"Hey, look!" Polly cried out. "There's one," and she pointed into the air. A tiny brown spot had emerged from a hole at the top of the wall, and it began to move across the ceiling like a bead on a string.

"That's a bug?" I asked. "*That? Where's* its legs?"

"It doesn't have any. It just slides on its stomach. Look, here comes the other one."

From the same hole another brown spot appeared and slid slowly toward the first. Then, just as their noses were about to touch, they suddenly pulled away, like the wrong ends of magnets.

"How come they do that?" I said. "How come they go up to each other like that and then move away?"

"That's how they say hello. They're going to kiss, but they change their minds because their breath smells bad. Look, they're dancing."

They did seem to be dancing—sliding back and

forth together, twirling around. "What makes them go like that?" I asked.

"There's wax up there," she said. "They're sliding on the wax."

"Wax! Who put *wax* up there?"

"I don't know. Somebody. Lots of people wax their ceilings. Like they wax floors."

I never know what to say when people tell lies like that. Usually I just pretend to believe them, but sometimes I try to argue. "Nobody does that," I said.

"They do so. There's this special wax that people use on their ceilings. Kings mostly. My teacher said. She read us a story once about this king who had a whole bunch of ceiling wax and all and he was always using it. For the bugs, probably, so they could dance."

"Kings don't wax their ceilings, and anyway, they don't have bugs." This wasn't what I wanted to be saying to my friend.

"This one did. My teacher told us. He had this special ceiling wax and he kept it in a little pot on his desk."

"A *king*?" I stared at her. "Oh, *sealing* wax, you mean. Polly, that's dumb. That's the dumbest thing I ever heard. You're thinking of sealing wax."

"Yeah. That's what I said."

"But not *that* kind of ceiling. The other kind. For sealing letters and stuff."

"They're both the same. Ask my teacher. Hey, M. E., I have an idea. You want to play bug race?"

"Bug race? What's that? You mean like potato race?"

"Potato race! There's no such thing. Potatoes can't run. Bug race is like horse race, except you don't use horses. Here's how we play: I pick a bug and then you pick the other one and whichever gets to the light first wins. You want to play?"

"I don't know. What happens if you lose?"

"*You* don't lose, the *bug* loses. You feel sorry for it, is all. We'll wait till they get lined up and then we'll start. I'll take that one and you can have the other one. Okay, GO!" she shouted, and somehow the two bugs began to move toward the light.

"What makes them go there," I asked, "to the light like that?"

"I don't know. They think it's the sun. They go there every day and just lie around without any clothes on, getting warm. That's how they get so brown. Then they go home. Hey, bug, MOVE!"

This time I didn't argue with her.

"MOVE!" she yelled again.

"I'll move when I please." Polly's grandmother was standing in the doorway behind us. "Get up off your back, Polly, and go to the store for me. I need more soap."

I lifted my head to look at her. She had taken her

apron off and she stood there in Polly's blouse and skirt. They fitted her better than they did Polly, and I realized all at once that they weren't Polly's clothes at all. They were her grandmother's. It was Polly who wore her grandmother's things. Not the other way around.

"POLLY!"

Polly didn't stir.

"Get up like I told you."

"Later," Polly said, but she spoke to the bugs on the ceiling. Her grandmother remained in the doorway for a while, and I thought she would yell, but she didn't. She didn't even sigh. She just turned back to the kitchen.

"She's always making me do stuff that she doesn't feel like doing herself," Polly said to me.

"Maybe it's because she's old," I said.

"Yeah. Old people are terrible, don't you think? They shouldn't let old people be born."

I turned to her and smiled, happy to be there, happy to listen to the things she said, happy to have her as my best friend. She didn't tell lies, really. She just said crazy things. Or dumb ones. It didn't matter which. "When this is over," I said, "let's go to your room and you can show me your things."

"I don't have any things," Polly said. "And anyway, this is my room."

"This? I thought this was the living room."

"It is. It's my bedroom, too, and my grandma's."

I looked around. "Then what's that down the hall?"

"The bathroom."

"That's it? That's the whole apartment?"

"Yeah. It's crummy, but it's better than where I used to live. I used to have to share a room with my sister. She always had the best bed and everything. All her stuff was better than mine. Here I have the best bed."

"Where is it?" I asked. "Your bed?"

"Over there. With the red pillows," and she pointed to the sofa behind us. It was like the bed Wanda and I might have had when we played poor children—hard-looking and full of lumps. "That's nice," I said. "That's a nice bed," and that was a nice thing to say to a friend, too.

CHAPTER TWENTY-FIVE

All the girls at Agnes Daly, except me, have what they call outside friends. An outside friend is someone who doesn't go to your school and is a better friend than anyone else you know. When you play with her you think up things to do that would never occur to you with your ordinary friends. In fact, you don't even think them up. They just happen.

"I had this really great time with my outside friend yesterday," Rhoda will say, and then she'll describe an afternoon that could have happened to nobody else in the world. "I was visiting her in this enormous house where she lives, and all of a sudden we decided to be Siamese twins. Just like that." That's the way things happen with outside friends: just like that. "So we dressed up in her father's huge T-shirt and her grandmother's long skirt and we tied our inside legs together and hopped all around the block. One kid thought we were for real." And I will listen and wonder why things like that never happen to me.

Now, though, I had an outside friend. "My outside friend and I did this wonderful thing," I could say to Rhoda or to Iris some day when I went back to school. "She lives with her grandmother in this really funny place where they have huge old sofas for beds and there are these special bugs that stick to the ceiling. They put on shows, and we were watching them for a while, when all of a sudden we decided that they were racing bugs. We spent the whole morning just lying on our backs picking which one would win."

"You better yell at your bug," Polly said, "so it'll move."

It *was* moving. It was within an inch of the light bulbs, in fact, while Polly's was far behind. Anyway, I felt silly, yelling at a bug. "I'll yell in my head," I said.

"Morton yells out loud."

I sat up. Morton? "Morton plays this? Morton plays bug race with you? I thought you just made this up." *That's* what they did? Lay here on the floor, just as she and I were now lying, and raced bugs? Did she tell him about ceiling wax, too, and about how bugs said hello and got brown in the light of a bulb? "Who wins?" I asked. "You or him? His bug, I mean, or yours?"

"Mine."

"All the time? Yours always wins?"

"Yeah."

"How come?" I asked, although I already knew how come: Morton never wins anything. Not even Bingo, where you don't have to be smart. Not even War. I never have to cheat to win when I play with him, because no matter what happens, he loses all the time. "Think about what you're doing, Morton," my mother says to him, even when we're playing War and thinking doesn't do any good. Then she says "He would" to her listener when he loses all his cards.

"Because I can make bugs do whatever I want. I'm magic. GO!" she yelled, and suddenly her bug moved away from its spot on the ceiling and began to catch up with mine. "GO!" I yelled at my own bug. "MOVE!" but it stopped in its path and remained fixed, like a pin stuck through paper, while Polly's glided past and bumped its head on the ring of bulbs.

"See? He won! My bug won!" She got to her feet and jumped up and down. "Good bug. GOOD BUG! See, M. E.? I told you I was magic."

"You are not. It's just luck. And anyway, I don't care. It's just a game," but I did care. I felt sorry, just as Polly said I would, for my bug, standing still up there, too dumb to move. And I felt sorry for myself;

usually I won things. I felt sorry for Morton, too, who lost all the time.

"Put the seven green sticks in one bundle," my mother was saying. "No, *seven*. Count them out. Now make another bundle just like that one. Make six bundles in all."

They were sitting at the kitchen table, and although it was still early evening the overhead light was on, because the sun came into the room only in the morning. I walked around them on my way to the window, and Morton looked up as I passed him, but my mother didn't.

"You now have six bundles of seven. Six sevens. That means six times seven. Six times seven equals what, Morton?"

A tree grew up from the courtyard below, and in the summer you could lift up the window screen and touch its leaves. I did that now, pulling leaves off one after another and letting them float away like paper planes. No one ever went into the courtyard, because there was no way to get inside except through the cellar, and besides, everybody from the building could look down at you once you were there. Still, there were two benches facing each other, and now and then pigeons rested on them—fat, silent pigeons in dark-gray coats, who tipped their heads to one another and left thick white stains when they flew away.

"I can't hear you, Morton."

One leaf landed on a bench, making no sound.

"Six times seven equals," he said, and I felt his eyes on my back.

"Equals what, Morton? Equals *what*? Count the bundles. Count by sevens. Ready? Begin. Seven. Fourteen. Now, what comes after fourteen?"

In another moment, Morton was going to say something dumb and my mother was going to say "Stupid" to her listener on the wall.

"Hey, guess what." I turned around from the window before Morton had a chance to answer anything at all. "Guess what happened today? I was playing this game with Polly and I was ahead the whole time and then something happened and I lost. I lost the whole game."

My mother looked up at me. "That's too bad, Mary Ella," she said. "What game was it?"

"It was a race, and I lost. I lost the whole race."

"Well, try harder next time. Count by sevens, Morton. Seven. Fourteen. What comes after fourteen?"

"Fifteen."

"Be quiet, Mary Ella."

"Fifteen," Morton said.

CHAPTER TWENTY-SIX

Ever since Aunt Sophia died, I think about how surprised she'd be if she came back all of a sudden and saw all the changes that have happened in the world since her funeral. Like those fancy new buses with the bodies that bend, and those toothbrushes that play music when you scrub them on your teeth. Sometimes I pretend that she's with me when I walk down the street, and I show her things that have changed. "Look at the new cars, Aunt Sophia," I tell her, "with those funny bumpers and everything. And we have these new streetlights now that go on by themselves when it gets dark. And look at these TVs," I say, pausing at a store window. "You can play games with them and everything." I can feel her eyes grow large as she watches. "Imagine that," she says. "Who would have thought?"

Mostly now, though, she'd be surprised at the changes in *me*.

"Look out, Mary Ella," my mother cried out, and she pushed her chair quickly from the table.

"She spilled her milk," Morton said in surprise, as a white puddle spread from plate to plate, soaking the napkins and coating the spoons. "Mary Ella spilled her milk!"

"I don't know how it happened," I said, jumping up. "It went over so fast," but that wasn't true. It had taken me a long time to knock it over. I had started very slowly, leaning the edge of my hand against the glass until it began to travel a small path across the table. The milk splashed in waves from side to side, but it wouldn't spill out. Why was it so hard to knock over a glass of milk? I bumped my plate into it once, and when that didn't work, I picked it up and dropped it on its side.

"Look out!" my mother cried.

"Mary Ella spilled her milk!" Morton had never seen that happen before. "Look what it's doing. It's making a big J. Look what Mary Ella did, Mom. The milk is getting all over the table."

"It was an accident, Morton," my mother explained. "We all have accidents," and my father rushed over with a rag to catch the spreading puddle before it hit the floor.

I didn't spill my milk every night, but I spilled it a lot after that, and soon I got so I could spill it without even trying. Sometimes even when I was trying not to.

"Be careful tonight, Mary Ella," my mother would say. "Don't spill," and I *would* be careful, picking up the glass with both hands, holding it tight, fastening my eyes on its rim, the way Morton does, and lifting it slowly to my mouth. Then, just as it would reach my lips, my elbow would twitch or my wrist give out, and a sudden splash would hit my lap and trickle, strangely cold, between my thighs.

Once, Morton and I spilled our milk at the same time. I pushed my glass across the table as I saw his go down, and they toppled over together, like a couple of clowns, rolling side by side in a fat white ring.

"Mary Ella, don't do that," but it was Morton who spoke, not my mother or my father. "You're not sup- posed to do that."

The thing was that although I did a lot of dumb things this summer—one dumb thing after another until I became just like Morton—my mother didn't seem to mind or even to notice. "Soak it in the sink awhile," she had said when I showed her my blouse with the tar on its front. And when I brought it to her again the next morning, she didn't say anything at all.

By then, though, she had seen Morton's report card. "Look," he had said, coming in to breakfast. "I have something to show you," and he handed her the envelope with his name written in beautiful script. "I got O in conduct."

"Very nice," she said, slipping the report card into her hand. "Very nice," and then she saw the seven at the bottom of the page, and after that she said nothing at all, not even to her listener.

The silence that fell over her passed from one of us to the other like a bad cold, and like a cold, it stayed with us wherever we went: to the Laundromat, to the supermarket, to the park where we took our Sunday walk. All summer long she was angry at everything he did, even though by then I was doing the same dumb things.

Dumber, even.

Every day before I went upstairs for supper, I would stretch out the front of my T-shirt and fill it with matchbooks picked up from the street, or from trash cans or the stream that ran along the curb. They were dirtier than the things Morton collected, and more dangerous, too: Some had rows of matches tucked inside—unstruck matches, their pink heads rough against my thumb.

When I got them to my room, I'd dump them on my bed and sort them out. The restaurant ones went in one pile, the supermarket ones went in another, and the animal and flower ones went in a third. "Look," I said to my mother. "I'm starting a collection. It's going to be of matchbooks," and I waited for her to tell me that they were dirty, that they were dangerous, that I could start a fire, but she didn't say any of that. "Oh, look, Mary Ella," she said, lifting one up. "Did you see this? It's from a place in England," and she put it carefully beside the others, in the right pile.

And when I didn't get her a present for her birthday, it didn't seem to bother her at all.

"What are you going to get her?" Morton asked one day. He was holding something behind his back and he sounded excited as he stood in my doorway.

"Get who?"

"*You* know, Mary Ella," he answered, sounding impatient. "It's tomorrow. I'm getting her this lanyard I made in Creative Recreation. It could be for a belt."

For two weeks now I had been making myself forget my mother's birthday, just so I could see what it was like to wake up one morning and suddenly remember, too late, that I had nothing to give. I had tried to mix the days up in my head, so I wouldn't know when July nineteenth came, and I made myself think of other things all day, but it really didn't work. Two years ago I tried to forget my own birthday, so I'd be surprised when it finally arrived, but my mother spoiled it by telling me every day, "In six days"—or five, or four— "you'll be nine years old, and by then I will expect you to wash your hair by yourself instead of having me do it for you." Probably, though, I would have remembered anyway. Nobody forgets their own birthday. And besides, you can't make yourself forget anything. The more you try, the more you think about it; I knew as soon as Morton came to my room what he would say.

"*You* know, Mary Ella. It's tomorrow."

"I don't know what you're talking about," I said, and I closed the door before he could tell me.

I gave my mother a handmade card the next day, and that was all. It was a terrible card, with a picture of a girl standing in front of a house. The crayon went out of the lines all over the place, and the house was the kind that Morton draws, with a triangle roof and a tilted chimney. I put it on the kitchen table next to Morton's present so my mother would see them both when she came in.

"Very nice," she said, picking up the card and putting it down again. "Very nice," she repeated, and she began to unwrap the lanyard.

"Oh, my!" she said, and she held it up so it dangled from her fingers. "Isn't that nice!"

"You're supposed to wear it," Morton told her. "It's for a belt." He looked happy.

"Yes, I see," she said, and she tied it around her waist. "It's very pretty, Mary Ella."

"It's from Morton," I told her. "I just gave you the card."

"You did? Oh, I thought . . ." She picked the card up again and studied it carefully. "Why does it just say 'From me' on it?"

"It doesn't. It says M. E. That's what people call me now."

"Oh, I didn't know. It's a very nice card, Mary Ella," she said, even though it was terrible.

"I didn't remember to get you anything else," I said. "I forgot your birthday was today."

"No, you didn't," Morton said. "I told you."

"I didn't hear."

"It's all right," my mother said. "The card is really very pretty, Mary Ella. I like the colors." She held it out in front of her and looked at it for a long time, holding her head to one side, the way I had wanted her to look at my picture of the daisies. "It's just *lovely!*"

she said, at last sounding like the mother rabbit in the egg. "Lovely," she said, for the first time ever, but she said it because she was sorry for me, because she thought I had forgotten her birthday and had made the card in a hurry. Not because the card was lovely at all; it was terrible.

Only Morton was disappointed. "Why didn't you give her something nice?" he asked later. "You always give nice things."

The tar never came out of our shirts, Morton's or mine, and in the end my mother took them both away. She dropped mine into the clothing bin outside the supermarket, because poor children would be glad to have it, and she turned Morton's into a dustrag. A floor mop now wears the gray Mickey Mouse shirt with the tar fish on the stomach, and once a week it slides around under the bed, along the baseboards, up on the ceiling even, collecting things that no one else wants: dust puffs, pins, and cobwebs sticky with grime.

CHAPTER TWENTY-SEVEN

"You want to be in my club?" Polly asked one day.

I turned to look at her. "Be in your club?" Nobody had ever said that to me. The girls in my class are always asking each other to join clubs that they make up, but they never ask me. They have a lunch club and a walking club and a hair club. All they do at the lunch club is sit at the same table in the lunchroom, and all they do for the walking club is walk to school together. For the hair club they meet in the bathroom and comb their hair at the same time. And although I sometimes sit at the lunch table with them or comb my hair in front of the same mirror in the bathroom, I'm not in any of their clubs.

"What kind of club?" I asked Polly. We were sitting side by side under the awning, on the same curb where, in the beginning of the summer, I had sat alone, pretending the new girl would be my best friend. Now she was.

"No kind. It's just a club."

"Who else is in it?"

"No one. I just started it."

"Well, but what's it for?"

"It's so I can be president. You can be vice president if you like, in case I'm absent."

"But what do you *do?*" I asked. "I mean, do you walk somewhere or comb your hair, or what?"

"We don't do anything. We're just *in* it. You want to join? Morton's joined."

I looked at her again. "I thought you said no one else was in it."

"He's in my other club. I have two clubs."

"Who else is in that one?"

"No one. I just started that one, too. Last week. You want to join? All's you have to do is a trick I make up, and then you're a member."

I waited a long moment before answering. "What trick? An initiation, you mean?"

"A what?"

"Initiation. That's a trick you do to get into a club."

"There's a name for that? Well, your initiation could be you steal something."

"No."

"My sister did. We had this club once and she had to steal a beach chair from the five-and-ten. It was easy. She just walked in and put it on top of her head and walked out again. Nobody said anything. They thought it was her hat. It was a nice chair, with a thing to put your feet up on and everything. We used it for the president. You could steal a chair, if you wanted, and then you could sit in it when the president was absent."

A thin stream of water was running along the street against the curb, and I put my finger in it to make a little dam.

"You want to?"

"No."

"Then *what*? You want to climb something? That fence across the street? You want to climb that? You could walk on top of it for a little ways, and then pick a leaf from the top of that bush and eat it. That could be your trick."

"Polly, that fence has *spikes* on it."

"Yeah, well. How about that tree, then, down at the corner, with the pollynoses? You could climb to the top and put a pollynose on and climb back down again."

"No."

"Well, what then? This awning? You want to climb this awning? All's you have to do is slide on your stomach until you get to the wall. Then stand up and write your name under that window with some chalk and walk back, no fair using hands. It'll be easy. You can climb up there from that car roof."

I tilted my head back and looked up at the gray-green canvas stretched tight across its frame. It was thin and frayed, and here and there little points of light shone through its holes, like stars on a paper chart that you hold against the sky. Walk on *that*? "There's nothing to hold on to," I said.

"Yes, there is. Hold on to those bars, with your feet."

"With my *feet*? That's crazy. And anyway, you're not supposed to write on that wall. It's against the law or something."

"No, it's not. I write on walls all the time and nobody ever put me in jail. Besides, it's nice, writing on walls. When you go away, it's still there. It's like leaving yourself behind, for everyone to see."

"You're not supposed to," I said again, and after that we were silent a long time. I lifted my finger from the running stream and let some drips trickle down my leg and collect at the top of my sock, turning it gray, and then I thought of something. "Hey," I said. "What about *you*? What trick are you going to do for initiation?"

"Me? Nothing. I'm already *in* the club. Come on,

M. E. Then you can be a member. Like Morton. You can use this piece of chalk. It's brand-new."

I thought of something else: "What did Morton do," I asked, "for his trick?"

She paused a while before answering. "He went into that cellar. The one over there, with the little door."

I stared at her. Morton had gone in *there*? Where the old man lived and the rats ran around? So he could be in Polly's club? "What did he have to do when he was down there?" I asked, "Write his name, or what?"

"He had to find something and bring it back."

"What did he find?"

"I don't know. A glove."

"A glove! Whose glove? The old man's?"

"Yeah, I guess. It was old. The tops were gone and everything so his fingers showed through."

Morton had gone into the cellar and never told. I thought about that. Morton had pushed his way through the black down there, with his hands held straight before him, as though he were blindfolded for a game, and his chin down low on his chest. Noises had come, from the rats and the old man, and smells, too, from rotten things. After a while his toe had bumped against something soft and flat, and he had patted the cellar floor with his hands so he could pick up whatever it was and take it back to Polly to show he had been there. How long had it been, I wondered, before he had brought it out into the sun and found it was only a glove he held and not the body of a rat? He had put it on, too, even though the wool smelled of rot and was stiff with dirt. He had slid his hand into its cuff and watched as his fingertips, like five bald heads, pushed through a row of raveled collars. "Look," he'd said, making them nod. "People."

"Let's see the chalk," I said, holding my hand out to Polly.

CHAPTER TWENTY-EIGHT

The edge of the awning frame reached only to my chest when I stood on the car roof, and Polly had to push against my feet to get me up the rest of the way. The chalk in my pocket pressed into my hip, and I shifted to one side so it wouldn't break. It *was* new, as she had said, still flat at each end and silky smooth.

"You're almost there!" Polly shouted, although I hadn't begun to move. "Write your name on the wall nice and big, so everyone can see it. Write M. E."

The wall at the other end was far away, farther than I had imagined—a mile or more—and I quickly lowered my head to gaze instead into the canvas that for the first time ever I could feel against my skin. Its color, so close to my eye, turned out to be not green at all, or even gray, but black, and its smell was not of canvas but of something else. An old coat, maybe, or a closet, and it settled in my mouth like a taste.

I held my eye for a moment to one of the holes and

peered down at the sidewalk. Spread on the shadow of the awning was the shadow of my own body. A shadow on top of a shadow, like the tower of shadows Polly had said you could make that time on the roof. One shadow and one shadow made two shadows, after all. If Polly stepped on it, I wondered, would her foot sink in, just a little?

I closed my eyes then and began to move. Inch by inch I went, like a blind lizard, bending my knees, straightening them again, scratching at the cloth with my nails, rubbing my chin. On and on, for a mile. More. I didn't know I had reached the wall until I hit it with my head, and then I didn't know what to do next.

"Stand up!" Polly shouted from wherever she was. "Go ahead, M. E. Go *ahead!*"

In science class at Agnes Daly we watch a movie every year about evolution, where slimy things swim through a pool of water, and then, when they reach the shore, sprout legs and begin to crawl onto the land. After a while they rise up on their hands and knees, and finally they walk on their hind legs like apes. At the end a man in a bathing suit stands by himself on the beach. That's how I got up from my stomach, except at the end I wasn't on a beach. I was pressed against a wall of brick with my forehead at the sill of a second-story window.

"Hey, you made it!" Polly's voice came from far away. "What's it like up there?"

"Fine," I whispered into the brick.

"Write your name now. Write it just under the windowsill, where everybody can see it. Make it big."

A window slid open somewhere above and a shout was thrown from it. "You! YOU! You GIRL there! GET OFF THAT!" I pressed my hands into the wall. I had never noticed before how jagged brick was, or how full of color. All over there were patches of pink, or orange—purple, even. Black.

"GET AWAY FROM THERE!"

I flattened myself into my own shadow, stretching my neck, and suddenly I was looking into a living room. A stranger's living room, with furniture against the walls and things on the tables. Magazines and stuff. An open book. Lamps. A banana, halfway peeled, on a plate. There were shoes on the floor—somebody else's shoes, and I caught my breath, feeling like the giant girl who peered through my window each night. "Look!" I could say. "Look at the real sofa and the chairs. And the banana on the table." I could squeeze my arm through and move things around. Slip the shoes under the sofa, where they couldn't be seen. Pull the peel the rest of the way off the banana. Turn on the lamp.

At any moment, though, someone could walk in.

Someone—the lady who lived there—would remember the banana on the plate or the open book and, walking in, suddenly see my eyes over the sill. What would she do?

"What's she doing there?" someone cried out. The lady! A jump ran through my body. "How come she's up on the awning?" Someone had joined Polly on the sidewalk. A boy. Henry, probably. Then more voices came.

"How'd she get up there?"

"How's she going to get down?"

They spoke as though I couldn't hear them, and I felt like a performer in a show. At the circus, it could be, on the high wire.

"She's spying on someone, I bet. She's spying on those people who live there's apartment."

"She's going to climb in."

"She's going to rob them. Hey, Charles, look what Mary Ella's doing! She's going to rob that apartment."

"She's got something in her pocket."

"A gun!"

"No, it's a cigarette. She's going to smoke up there."

"It's a piece of *chalk*. Hey, she's writing something," and they began to call out the letters as though they were watching an airplane trail a message in the sky.

"T."

"H."

"I."

"S . . . This."

"Is."

"This is . . ."

"M."

"E."

"Apostrophe S. This is Me's . . ."

"A."

"W."

"N-I-N-G."

"This is Me's awning." They waited to see if there would be more.

"Me's awning?" somebody asked.

"She's crazy."

"No, she's not." It was Polly's voice now. "She's being initiated."

There was a silence.

"What?"

"Don't you know what initiated is? It's what you do to get into a club."

"What club?"

"Mine."

"She has to stand on the awning to get into a club? What kind of club is that?"

"HEY, GIRL. IF YOU DON'T GET OFF THERE I'M GOING TO CALL THE POLICE!"

"Somebody's going to call the police."

"She better get down."

"Look, she's turning around now. There she is. You can see her face."

"Look how dirty she got. Her clothes are all black."

"And her legs."

"Everything. Look at her *face*."

My back was against the wall now, and from the side of one eye I could see a crowd of faces. Everybody I knew was down there, but I didn't look at them long. I fastened my eyes instead on a wash bucket on the fire escape across the street. "*Spot!*" Miss Frazier always yells in Interpretive Dance. "Spot, and you won't fall."

"How's she going to get down?" somebody asked.

"Jump, probably."

"From *there?*"

"No, she's not," Polly said. "She's going to walk. Those are the rules. You have to walk to the front of the awning, no fair using hands, and then climb down."

"She's crazy." That sounded like Ezra.

"She's dumb." Justine. "Dumb like her brother."

CHAPTER TWENTY-NINE

Always, just before I fall, I can see the whole accident, even though it hasn't happened yet. I can see my ankle catch in the jump rope and my knees turn bloody even before it's my turn to jump, and I can see my hand miss the last rung of the monkey bars before I'm halfway across. Now, as I pressed my back against the brick wall, I could see my leg give way at the sound of some sudden noise—a car horn down the street or a window slamming shut—and I could see my body crash to the ground. I could hear it, too—I could hear the squawk of canvas as it ripped beneath my leg, and I could hear the hum of metal as my shoulder hit a bar.

I would end up like the girl in my make-believe game: in a wheelchair. I would be wheeled through the park with my legs wrapped in a blanket, even in summer, and a muffler at my neck.

Except this time, instead of saying, "She's gravely

ill," my mother would explain that I had broken my bones in a fall. "She had a terrible accident," she would say, but she wouldn't add that I had fallen from an awning or that I had gone up there because—because why? Because my best friend said I should. Because I did a dumb thing my friend told me to do.

Me, not Morton.

"Why doesn't she *move?*"

"She's too scared. Look at her leg shake."

"Come *on*, M. E. They're going to call the police."

"The fire department, too, I bet. They'll have to get her down with a ladder. Or one of those basket things."

"They don't send the fire department just to get somebody off an awning."

"They send them to get cats out of trees."

"No, they don't. That's just in baby books."

Or I would die. When I fell to the ground I would hit my head hard and then lie very still while everyone stood around me, afraid to come closer, afraid to move away. Later, the doorbell would ring, and my mother, answering it, would find Ina standing there, or Deirdre. There would be a tiny silence and in that moment my mother would know something terrible had happened. Morton, she would think, and Ina would say, "Mary Ella's hurt."

"Get down from there!" Somebody's mother was

coming up the block across the street. "Get down from there before you break your neck." It was Justine's mother, and I could see her now, from the side of my other eye, pulling a shopping cart loaded with bags. "Get down from there this *minute!*"

"She can't," somebody said. "She's too scared."

"Get off that thing," Justine's mother continued, "or I'll call your mother."

I held my head still, as though I were posing before a camera, and I kept my eyes on the wash bucket. "She's not home," I answered, lying, and I sent my words, one behind the other, over to the wash bucket, too. Even so, I swayed a little, and that's when the sudden noise came.

Justine's mother, seeing me sway, suddenly let go of her shopping cart, and a bag full of tin cans and jars hit the street like an explosion. My leg faltered, as I had known it would, and I pitched forward a little. The next thing I knew I was on the sidewalk.

"Look what you made me do!" Justine's mother was still shouting. Cans from her cart were rolling down the street, and a broken jar of something gray lay at her feet. Applesauce. "I'm going to tell your mother!" she yelled again, but I knew she never would. She didn't even know who my mother was, and besides, there was nothing to tell because nothing had really happened. The crash of the shopping cart had pushed

me like a spring away from the wall and sent me stum-
bling across the whole length of the awning. On my
feet! I hadn't crashed through the canvas. I hadn't
fallen to the ground. I hadn't even touched anything
with my hands. When I reached the front end of the
awning I had jumped down to the car and then to the
sidewalk. I had followed the rules. I could be in the
club. "Hey, Polly!" I shouted. "I did it! I did it, I did
it, I did it! I'm *initiated!* I wrote my name up there and
I walked all the way back, no hands! I can be in the
club!" I looked around. "Polly?"

"Hey, Mary Ella," Deirdre said. "How did you do
that?"

"I don't know," I answered. "Where's Polly?"

"I thought you were going to fall." She sounded
disappointed. They were all disappointed; as soon as
I landed on the sidewalk they began moving away.

"Me, too," I said, apologizing. "I thought I was going
to fall, too. It was an accident, sort of, that I didn't.
Where's Polly?" I asked again.

"I don't know. She was here before. I guess she went
home."

"Where's that glove you found?" I asked Morton.
"What?"
"You know," I said. "The glove from the cellar."
"The glove?"

"The glove you found in the *cellar!*"

"What?"

"THE GLOVE FROM THE CELLAR SO YOU COULD BE IN POLLY'S CLUB!"

"Oh," he said. "Wo-wo-wo-wo-wo," and he went to the hall closet. "You mean this one?" His voice settled into an overcoat, and in a moment he returned with a glove my father used to wear before he lost its mate. "You mean this?" he asked, handing it to me.

Probably I had known all along that Polly had made that up, about Morton and the cellar. There really was no glove. There was no club either, for Morton or for me. Polly had finally played a trick. Not on Morton, but on me, and I twisted the glove around in my hand for a long while. Then I did something I had never done before. I hit him. I hit Morton with the glove. Its fingers swept through the air and spread out like a real hand, covering his face with their slap. Then they curled into a little fist on the floor.

That was the one time I saw Morton cry.

AUGUST

CHAPTER THIRTY

And then, at last, my mother began to notice, and to mind. "What happened to your forehead?" she asked one afternoon.

"What forehead?"

"Why are you wearing that Band-Aid? What did you do to yourself?"

"Nothing. I just keep it there in case I need it for something. If I kept it in my pocket it would lose its stick."

"Take it off, Mary Ella. It looks ugly."

"I don't care. I like it."

I had been sitting alone on the living-room sofa, arranging my matchbooks in my lap, when she came home from work. "Where's Morton?" she asked next.

"At Polly's."

"Again? Day after day he plays with that girl."

"No, he doesn't," I told her. "He wasn't there Monday."

"Why does she play with him all the time, Mary Ella? She's *your* age."

"No, she's not," I answered. "She's younger."

There was silence for a while, and then, "Why are you just sitting here? Why aren't you doing anything?"

"I am doing something. I'm fixing up my matchbooks. Look," I said, holding one up, "a kangaroo."

"Throw those away, Mary Ella. It's dangerous to keep matches around the house. You could start a fire."

"I'm not collecting the matches. Just the covers. Look at this one. It's of a flower."

"Throw them away. They're dirty. You don't know where they've been."

"Yes, I do. They've been on the street."

"Throw them *away!*" Her voice rose a bit. "We have enough dirty things brought in here from the gutter."

"Some of them are from the sidewalk," I told her. I stood them in a row along the sofa arm. "I'm making a parade."

There was some more silence and then she said, "It isn't wholesome for a girl your age to sit around the house all day, not doing anything."

Our sofa is the kind that's made of plush, and it darkens when you draw your finger along it. I made a thick, fuzzy M alongside my thigh. "I didn't sit around all day," I answered. "I played with Polly in the morning."

"Why don't you spend some time on your writing?" *Your* writing, she always says. "You used to do such nice writing."

"I *am* writing," I answered, drawing the three bars of the E. "See?"

"Stop that, Mary Ella. That's bad for the upholstery. Why don't you write another essay? You wrote that lovely essay about Susan B. Anthony. Why don't you write another one? You could win another prize."

"It was Elizabeth Cady Stanton."

"Mary Ella, what's the *matter* with you? Why are you behaving like this all of a sudden? Spilling your milk and wearing dirty clothes. Letting your nose run. Not doing anything. Making yourself ugly."

"I don't know," I answered. "I don't know why I'm so ugly and everything." I drew another line across the sofa.

"*So* ugly," she corrected. "Don't say 'suh.' It sounds ignorant."

"*So* ugly. But you said once that it didn't matter if I was ugly. You said lots of ugly women get married."

"Stop being *fresh*! And pick your head up. Don't sit that way. You look just like your . . . STOP THAT, MARY ELLA!" I'd never heard her yell before. "You never used to behave like this. What's the matter with you?"

"I don't know," I said again.

I waited for her to say something else, but she just moved off into the hallway, and when I heard her speak at last, it wasn't to me at all. "Nasty brat," she said, or "rat." She was speaking to her listener, and for the first time ever she wasn't telling about Morton.

She was telling about me.

CHAPTER THIRTY-ONE

"Mary Ella?"

My mother had come into my room so quietly her voice made me jump.

"Mary Ella, I want to talk to you." She sat on my bed, which is something she never does. It makes the mattress sag, she says, and it wrinkles the bedspread.

"What about?" My matchbooks were spread all over the floor. I was taking out the doubles to give to Morton, and I was making a parade out of all the rest, standing them up on their edges, like tents, in a careful row against the wall.

"I thought I told you to throw those away. Look how dirty they are."

"I'm giving some of them to Morton. He's going to start a matchbook collection, too. Just like mine. So we can be twins."

"Never mind," she said, which isn't what I expected her to answer. "I didn't come to talk about that," she went on, but she didn't say what she had come to talk about. She just sat on my bed, where no one is supposed to sit, and stared down at my parade.

"Mary Ella," she finally began, "your father and I have been noticing your behavior lately, and we've been very dissatisfied with what we see. You've altered a lot since—since the beginning of the summer."

Since Polly came, is what she meant, and I waited for her to go on.

"So we've decided to . . ." She touched a matchbook with her toe, toppling it.

"To what?"

"To make some changes."

There was silence for a long time.

"Like what?"

"Mary Ella," she began again, "your father and I have given this a lot of thought." That's how she talks when she's about to say something terrible. "Your father," she says, instead of Daddy or Pop, and "We've given this a lot of thought," which means there's no use arguing. "We feel there is such a thing as a bad influence, and we have decided that it is time that you two were separated."

I looked up at her quickly. "Who two?" I asked, although I already knew. Polly was the bad influence. She got me to put a Band-Aid on my forehead when

I didn't need one, and to say "suh" instead of "so." She made me wear dirty clothes and spill my milk at the table. She tricked me into climbing the awning, although I didn't know if my mother knew about that. She made me look ugly. Now we weren't going to be allowed to play together, and I wondered if that meant Morton couldn't play with her anymore, either.

"Morton, too?" I asked.

She looked at me as though she were trying to make out my words. "Stop being fresh, Mary Ella. That's just the kind of behavior I'm talking about."

"I'm not being fresh. Can't Morton play with Polly either?"

"Polly? I'm not talking about Polly. I'm talking about you and Morton." She smoothed the bedspread alongside her lap. "Mary Ella, you are together too much. Your father and I both feel that you should be separated for a while."

Separated? Morton and me? *Separated?* Separated was what happened to kids in school who got into fights and Mr. Healy had to pull them apart. Separated was what happened to Iris and Rhoda when they talked too much in class. Separated was what happened to kids who had friends. "I'll have to separate you," the teacher says, as though they're Siamese twins, and Iris ends up having to sit next to me.

But Morton and I already were separated. We had separate rooms and we went to separate schools. We sat on separate sides of the kitchen table and we even played with Polly at separate times. "How separated?" I asked my mother, but when I looked at her I saw that she was crying—right out there in the open, not in the bathroom in front of the sink—and I suddenly understood what she meant.

She was going to send me away somewhere, to get me away from Morton. Because I gave him dirty stuff for his collections. Because I told him the wrong answers to his arithmetic problems. Because I was fresh and he could become fresh, too. Because I hit him in the face with a glove and made him cry.

Because *I* was the bad influence.

"You need to be apart, Mary Ella. For a little while."

Where would they send me? To a boarding school? To a *reform* school? Somebody on Polly's street had been sent to reform school last year, only they didn't call it that. They called it some kind of home.

"Where?" I asked now. It was the only word that came out of my mouth.

"We've found someplace nice, Mary Ella." She kept saying my name when she spoke to me. "It's a farm."

A farm! A *farm*? I was going to live on a farm with cows and things? With *chickens*? Instead of going to Agnes Daly in the fall I was going to live on some place with a bunch of animals? I gave my matchbook parade a kick with my toe and sent it sprawling across the floor.

"It's a very nice place," my mother went on.

"I don't want to hear about it," I said. "I DON'T WANT TO HEAR ABOUT IT!" I shouted so loud that she drew back on the bed, wrinkling the spread even more.

Each year in June, when Agnes Daly closes for the summer, all the girls buy new autograph books and pass them around for everyone else to sign. Mostly they write little puzzles, with numbers and letters instead of words: "2 SWEET 2 B 4-GOTTEN." Things like that. I made up a puzzle message of my own once, although I never got to put it in anybody's book because nobody asked me to sign. It went "I hope 2 C U in the fall." and I really did hope that, because I never knew in June whether I would return in September.

Each year, I have to wait until the middle of summer to see if I am going to get another scholarship, and some years, even if I do get my scholarship, I'm not sure I'll be going back. The summer after my father had to sell his bookstore there wasn't enough money for all the things the scholarship didn't pay for, and Aunt Sophia had to help. Now she's dead, though, and so I worry every year.

This year especially, because this was the year I most wanted to go back. I was going to be a lower senior, which is what they call a seventh grader at Agnes Daly, and that means lots of privileges. You get to work on the school paper, for one thing, and you get invited to tea once a week with Miss Rice, but best of all, you go to different rooms for some of your classes, instead of staying all day with one teacher, and your gym teacher is a man. Mr. Healy.

I don't know why I love Agnes Daly so much. I don't have any friends there, except for Wanda, and she isn't even in my class. She barely speaks to me, in fact, on the playground or in the lunchroom, and she sometimes even calls me "baby" to her friends, even though I'm a grade ahead of her. She's nice to me only when we're not in school. Also, I think you learn more in public school. Ina and Deirdre know a whole lot of things about geography and grammar that I never heard of, and Justine's arithmetic book is way ahead of ours, but I love Agnes Daly all the same.

I love the uniform and I love the classrooms and I even love Miss Rice and her lectures about the roof over our heads. I love the building, too. It's made of gray stone, and it has turrets and balconies and lots of stairways. It also has a hidden dumbwaiter that leads nowhere.

Joseph discovered the dumbwaiter one day when he came upon its only doorway in a storage closet off the art room. "Look at *this!*" he cried out, and we all left our easels to watch him tug at the small wooden door. Inside was a wooden shelf that moved up and down on ropes through a tower that smelled of old things. "It goes to a secret room," Iris said, and we all caught our breath. "There's a crazy man who lives up there," Rhoda said, "and this is how he gets his food."

We put a note on the dumbwaiter the next day and sent it up into the darkness, scalding our hands on the rope as it whizzed by and chilling our noses with the damp. "Here's a special message!" we shouted into the dark. The note was still on the dumbwaiter when we brought it down the next day, and it contained no reply, but that didn't matter, really. I was just happy knowing that our school had a dumbwaiter that no one had ever seen before, and a crazy man, maybe, who lived in an unseen room.

That's what I love about Agnes Daly, and that's why each summer I hope I won't have to go to P.S. 53, with its bare tile walls and linoleum floors.

Now I wasn't going to go to either one. I was going to a farm.

"When do I go?" I finally asked.

"Go where?" My mother looked into my face.

"To the farm."

"Oh, Mary Ella," and this time her face looked as I'd never seen it look before. As though someone had hit it. "It's not you who's going. It's Morton."

CHAPTER THIRTY-TWO

It was Morton, after all, who was the bad influence. Not Polly. Not me. Morton.

"You'll get good, wholesome food there," my mother told him the next day, "and farm-fresh milk. And you'll learn all about how a farm works. Mrs. Floyd will teach you how to milk cows and feed chickens, and you'll get to ride around in a tractor, maybe. It will be like going to camp, Morton." She made it sound like some kind of reward or something. "Would you like that?"

"Yes," Morton said.

"You'll go as soon as summer school is over. In two weeks. And of course we'll come and visit you whenever we can, and you'll come home for holidays, and in the meantime we'll write to you and you can write to us. You'll get lots of mail, Morton. Won't that be nice?"

I'd never heard her talk to him like that before.

Usually when she wants him to do something he doesn't want to do, she just tells him to do it and he does.

"And there'll be a special school for you to go to, Morton, where the work will be a little easier for you, and there'll be other children your age who also have problems with their schoolwork."

A dumb kids' school.

"And then in January we'll see how you like it, and if you want to stay longer you may."

Two weeks later, all his clothes were set out in little piles on his bed: the Mickey Mouse shirts, the under-wear, the socks, the shorts, the pants—all laid out in a big oblong, following the border of his bedspread. "Look, Mary Ella," he said. "Look, Mom. I made a design."

On the pillow were his three bags of collections.

"You can't take those with you," my mother said. "Mrs. Floyd isn't going to want all that junk in her house."

"But I need them," he said.

"No, Morton. There won't be room."

"I'll keep them under my bed."

"No. Find something else to take. Something small."

"What?"

"I don't *know*, Morton. *Find* something. A picture

would be nice," and that evening the bags of collections were back in Morton's closet.

"Morton's going away tomorrow," I said to Polly. We were both lying on the floor, watching the bugs on the ceiling. They were moving in straight, steady lines away from the light bulbs, and they looked like cars seen from a tall building. "He's all packed and everything. My mother's going to take him to the bus tomorrow at six o'clock in the morning." I had to whisper because her grandmother was asleep on the sofa.

"Six o'clock in the morning? That's when the bus leaves? Six o'clock in the morning is still *night*."

"Yeah. It has to leave early because it's a long trip."

"Hey, M. E., let's give him a going-away present," Polly said. "Let's give him those bugs to take with him. They can be his pets. He can put them on his ceiling and he can talk to them at night when everybody else is asleep."

"Polly, he can't do that," I said, but I wondered all the same. Bugs were small. Morton could take them instead of his collections. He could put them on the ceiling, as Polly had said, and talk to them while he lay far away in the dark of a room he had never seen before.

[245]

"Okay," I said. "Let's."

Polly brought in a broom from the kitchen and, holding it upside down, swept both bugs into its bristles.

They did have legs after all: short, whiskery threads that thrashed around when we held them upside down in our palms. "Look," Polly said, nudging one with a fingernail. "They're ticklish."

"Who's that?" Polly's grandmother woke up suddenly and turned to us.

"It's me," Polly said.

"No, the other one."

"That's M. E."

"Who?" She sat up slowly.

"Mary Ella. Morton's sister."

"Oh, her. Hello, Mary Ella. It didn't look like you at first, all dressed up like that. You going somewheres, to a party or something?"

"No."

"Then why is your hair combed?"

My hair *was* combed, and I was wearing clean clothes, too. I had started taking baths again, and I wiped my nose when it ran. Also, I had stopped spilling my milk. Maybe, I thought, my parents would decide that Morton wasn't a bad influence on me after all. Maybe they wouldn't send him away.

"What do bugs eat?" Polly asked her grandmother.

"Depends what kind you have. Some eat sweaters. Some eat houses. Some eat behind your ears."

"These." Polly held out her hand.

"What do you want to feed *them* for? They already ate. Look how fat they are."

"We're giving them to Morton for a present," Polly told her. "He's going away tomorrow. To a farm. To live."

"A bug farm?"

"No, Grandma. A farm with cows and chickens. I told you that already. What do these bugs eat?"

Her grandmother poked at them with a finger. "Gingersnaps," she said. "Gingersnaps is what they like. Lots of spice."

Polly punched some holes in an empty Jell-O box and dropped the bugs into it, along with some gingersnap crumbs. "Maybe they're the kind of bugs that carry messages," she said. "You know? You tie a note on their leg and they fly home with it? Morton could send us special messages and stuff."

"That's pigeons. And anyway, these bugs can't fly."

"Crawl, then."

Morton wasn't home from summer school when we got back to my apartment, and we stood in the doorway of his empty room for a while, holding on to the Jell-O box and looking at the suitcase that lay open on his bed. It was all packed now, and the clothes made a smooth mound, like somebody's stomach, under a Snoopy shirt. His school shoes lay on the floor, one upside down, one on its side, trailing their laces behind them.

"Let's put the bug box on top of his clothes," I said, "so he'll see it as soon as he comes in," but Polly didn't seem to hear. She was walking around his room, picking things up, putting them down again. Looking for something. In another moment she was on her hands and knees, sliding Morton's train box out from under his bed.

"What are you doing?" I demanded. The lid was off now and I stared into the box. All the train cars were tucked into their special cutouts, except for the coal car, whose space lay empty and full of shadow.

"Let's take the bugs for a ride," she said. "We'll get them used to traveling so they won't throw up to-morrow in the bus, like I did." She lifted out a red boxcar from the train box and slid open its door. "Let's put them in here. What's that mean, C & O?"

"Chesapeake & Ohio."

"Okay, that'll be their names. This one is Chesa-peake," she said, dropping one of the bugs inside, "and this one's Ohio." She closed the little door and wheeled the car back and forth across the floor.

Someone across the courtyard was listening to a ball

game, and a cheer suddenly floated from a window and into Morton's room. "That was a home run," Polly said. "Everybody yells like that when there's a home run, even when it's not their team. It makes them happy, like it's their own home and somebody's come back to it, all safe."

"Yeah," I answered, but I really wasn't listening much. "Polly," I said, and I asked something I had been wanting to ask for two weeks. "Are you sorry Morton is going away? Will you miss him?"

"Me? No. I never miss anybody."

Not even me? I wanted to ask. Would you miss me, if I had to go away? Instead, I said, "Not even your mother? Or your sister?"

"No." She opened the boxcar door again and looked in. "Hey, Chesapeake's doing exercises in there. Look, M. E., he's lying on his back and making his feet move up and down."

"Do they miss you?" I persisted. "Do they write to you?"

"Sometimes. They moved to a new place. My sister has to go to a new school. You know what? Where they live now it's an hour earlier than it is here."

"That's how far away they live?"

"Yeah. Anything that happens here, it doesn't happen there until an hour later. Like that home run. Where my mother lives, it won't happen for another hour, because it's only a quarter till four there," she said, looking at Morton's clock, "instead of a quarter till five."

"Polly, that's dumb. That's really dumb. That home run has already been *made*."

"Not where my mother lives. It has to wait another hour. Also, sometimes it isn't even today there. It's still yesterday."

And then suddenly, something she had just said made me stop still. "Polly," I whispered. "It's a quarter to five? A quarter to *five*?" I stared at her awhile. "Where's Morton? How come he's not home?"

CHAPTER THIRTY-THREE

We tried the movie theater first. After that we went to the candy store and the five-and-ten and the barbershop. Places he never goes, but I couldn't think of where he *did* go. Finally, we went to his school, looking into doorways along the way, and asking kids if they had seen him. I felt funny telling them that he was missing again, scaring them for nothing, like the last time, and so I pretended that he wasn't missing at all; we were just looking for him.

Ina thought she had seen him, but she couldn't remember where, and anyway she wasn't sure if it was yesterday or today. Franklin saw him right then. "There," he said, pointing to a small figure two blocks away, but it turned out to be somebody else. A small old man.

The school building was quiet and still, like those photographs of famous monuments where, mysteriously, nobody is in sight, even though it's daytime. I knew from a block away that the doors would all be locked and the windows closed tight. Polly and I stood at the bottom of the steps a long while, looking into their silence. A name had been spray-painted near the door: RODNEY, it said, in white letters all crowded together and puffed out like pillows. Polly ran up the stairs to write LOVES POLLY under it with her chalk, and then she surrounded both names with a heart. She stepped back and smiled at the door. "Look, M. E.," she said. "He loves me. Rodney loves me."

"Polly, where *is* he?"

"I don't know. I've never even met him."

"No, I mean Morton. Where did he *go*?"

"Morton? I don't know. Somewhere. He's getting something, probably."

"Where were you?" My mother was waiting for me in the doorway. She was wearing the slippers she puts on sometimes when she comes home, and her hair was wet with sweat. She looked messy. "I wanted Morton home early today so he could get ready. Where is he?"

"I don't know," I answered. "He didn't come home from school." The words, coming suddenly into my ears, made my head shiver. "Polly and I just came back from looking for him," I added, so she would know it wasn't my fault. "We went to his school and the movies and everything."

"He didn't come home from school?" I don't think she heard what I'd just said.

"No." And then I said, "He's probably hiding someplace. He does that. Remember that time?" He *had* hidden once—behind a tree in the park while we were all sitting on the grass. After a while he came out and said, "Surprise!" but none of us had noticed he'd been away.

"Hiding! Hiding from what?"

"I don't know. Maybe he felt like it," and suddenly I began to believe that myself. "Maybe he doesn't want to go to the farm tomorrow."

She didn't seem to hear that, either, and in the next moment she was out the door. She was still wearing her slippers.

Maybe he was hiding right there in the apartment, behind a door somewhere, in a closet, in *his* closet. "Morton?" I called into the hall. "Morton?" I said into his room. "I know you're there," I whispered into his closet door, just as I do when I'm "It" in hide-and-seek: *I know you're there*, I say through a door, and the next moment, among a tangle of clothes and shoes, I see the arms and legs and face of someone I know.

I pulled on the knob. Morton's three bags of collections stood on the floor, one beside the other, and a little puff of dust scurried by. Otherwise, the closet was empty. His clothes had all been packed away.

I walked back into the kitchen and stared into the courtyard. "Morton?" I called, blowing his name through the window screen. "Morton?" although I knew he wasn't there. Who would hide in the courtyard, where everyone could see?

Dinner was already cooking and something from a pot sent down trickles that sizzled on the stove. I lifted the lid and looked inside. Chili. We never had chili in the summer, but that was Morton's favorite supper. Maybe my mother was making it just for him, because it was his last night home, and I wondered if she was sorry he was going away.

I stirred the pot awhile with a spoon, and suddenly I knew Morton would come back. If his dinner was there, then *he* would be there, too, to eat it. He was coming up the sidewalk right now, in fact, with my mother. She was a little ahead, hurrying in her slippers, and he was sliding his shoes along behind her. Past the fire hydrant, past one doorway, past another, another, another. Now they were at the awning, and my mother was getting out her key. I counted their steps across the lobby floor and then up the first flight of stairs, the second, the third. They were coming to our own door now, and I waited for the key in the lock. When I didn't hear it, when I didn't hear anything at all, I started them again from the sidewalk, farther back this time.

I'll set the table, I decided. I'll set the table for Morton and everybody, and I'll set it very slowly— fork by fork and spoon by spoon—and as soon as I'm through they'll be back. "You were right," my mother would say. "He was hiding." Morton would be pale from staying in the dark so long, and his clothes would be wrinkled. He'd look at me on his way to the bathroom. "Mom still has her slippers on," he'd say. Maybe later, when we were all at the table, we would laugh, the way I do sometimes when I'm scared about something, and then I'm not anymore.

I set Morton's place at the table very carefully, running my finger an extra time along the crease in his napkin and then resting a fork in its exact center. Next to that I put his dinner plate, turning it so that the big flower on the border was where the twelve would be if it were a clock, and I set his milk glass right above that. I set all the other places, too, nicely. Then, the moment I put down the last glass, the door opened, just as I knew it would, and someone came in.

"Where is everybody?" It was my father. "Why are you here alone?"

"I'm setting the table," I said, "while Mom gets Morton. He's hiding."

"Hiding!" He looked into my face, at my mother's empty chair, at Morton's. "What do you mean, hiding?"

"He does that sometimes," I said. "Remember that day in the park?"

"Where is he? Hiding where?"

"I'm not sure. Somewhere. Mom went to find him."

"How long has he been gone? When did he leave?"

"I don't know." And then, "He didn't come home from school." And because the words didn't come out at first, I ended up saying them too loud, shouting them, almost.

"He didn't come home from school? Where *is* he? Why didn't you call me? Why didn't you call the police?"

The police! The word made something squeeze the sides of my head.

"Why didn't you?"

"I don't know." I didn't want to tell him I hadn't noticed until a quarter to five that Morton was late coming home from school. "He's just hiding," I said. "Mom's bringing him back. His place is all set at the table and everything, and his supper is waiting."

My father walked through the living room and into

Morton's room. "His shoes are here," he called out. "How did his shoes get here if he didn't come home from school?"

"His shoes?" I asked, following him.

"What are his shoes doing here?" He was shouting now, and he looked angry.

I looked at the two brown shoes, the ones Morton wore to school every day, with the scratches at the toe, and the laces that came untied all the time.

"I guess he took them off," I said, and I bent down to line them up neatly, one beside the other, and tuck their laces inside. "He just put them here after he took them off," I said, looking up at my father, who was pulling at his hair now.

And then the front door opened and my mother came in. Alone. She looked at us both without speaking.

"His shoes are here," my father said.

"His shoes?" My mother stared down at the floor. "Who put his shoes here?"

"*He* did," my father shouted. "Who else? He came home after school and he took his shoes off. Then he went out again."

"But where would he go without his shoes?"

"NOWHERE!" I had never heard my father shout like that before. "He put on some *other* shoes."

"What other shoes?"

"How should I know? How many pairs of shoes does he have? Sneakers or something."

"But why would he do that?" She was beginning to shout now too.

"I DON'T KNOW!"

It was a long time before I finally spoke, and when I did it was in a whisper. "I know," I said, not looking at either of them. "I know where he is," and I ran past them out the door.

I had known all along.

I, too, had seen his shoes. I had seen them when I first entered his room with Polly, and all afternoon, walking with her to the movie theater, to the five-and-ten, to the barbershop, to the school, I knew somewhere inside my head or my stomach or wherever it is that you know things like that, that Morton had gone up to the roof in his sneakers so he could climb over the wall. Polly had been right—he had gone to get something. He had gone to get his train car so he could take it with him to the farm. Instead of his collections.

I stood still a moment and tried to catch my breath before I reached the top step. It was twilight by then, and the sun, deep orange now and flat, shone through the open door. It rested on top of the far wall like a coin on edge. With one finger I could have sent it rolling to the corner and crashing over the side.

The floor glowed orange in the light, and ripples I had never seen made shadows on the tar. Chimney pipes made shadows, too—long black shadows, flat as paint. I stood a long moment in the doorway, looking at the sun, at the shadows, at the ripples on the floor. *I know you're there!* I whispered to myself. *I know you're there!* I said when at last I sank my foot into the warm orange tar. *I know you're there!* when I edged very slowly to the wall on my left. "I know you're there!" I shouted as I reached the edge of the roof, and there he was.

CHAPTER THIRTY-FOUR

What is it like, I wondered, to be unconscious? "What's it like?" I asked the nurse. "Does he know I'm here? Can he hear me? Can he feel my hand?" I pushed aside his hospital gown and pressed a dent into his shoulder, as though it were a lump of clay. "Can he feel that?"

"It's like being asleep," she answered—but it's not. When you're asleep and someone presses a dent in your shoulder, you open your eyes, and when someone calls your name you answer "What?"

When you're asleep you wake up.

"Does he dream?" I asked. "If it's like being asleep, does he have dreams? Is he dreaming now?" Was he? I wondered. Was there, behind his closed eyelids, a whole crowd of things making a story he could watch? Did the sounds of the room—the rattle of bottles in the tray beside his bed, the rustle of my clothes as I walked across the floor—occur inside his dream as something else: bottle caps or trains or sailboats on a lake?

"Morton," I said aloud, "it's me. Mary Ella," and I wondered if, in his dream, my words became those of someone else—a beautiful lady, maybe. "Here's some pretty flowers," I said for her, and I fluttered my fingers at his face. "They're for you," and I waited for the figure in the dream behind his lids to press a bowl of roses to his nose.

Or did he dream, instead, about his fall? Did he, as he lay there so still, watch the accident happen over and over again? Did the rattles and the rustles in the room become the wings of startled pigeons and the sound of his very own scream?

"Morton?" I reached out and touched his lashes, and then I did a crazy thing. "Let me watch with you," I said, and I lifted up his lids so I could look inside, so I could see, with him, that afternoon on the rooftop when he tried to get his coal car and he toppled from the wall.

"Look out!" the nurse cried. "What are you doing?" and I dropped my hand.

"Does he dream?" I asked.

"Don't do that to him."

"Does he?" I insisted.

"We don't know," she finally answered. "Probably not."

What was it *like*? What was it like not to know that it was day, that it was night? That the sun was on your face, that it wasn't? That sometimes a man in orange coveralls hung outside your window and wiped it with a cloth?

I thought all at once of the princess in that fairy tale, the one who snagged her thumb on a spindle or something and went to sleep for a hundred years. A hundred *years* she lay asleep! while everything around her stirred and changed. Vines, for instance. Long vines, like quiet thieves, crept under all the window-panes, entering rooms where they had never been allowed, fingering things that weren't theirs. And trees. Trees grew where there had been no trees at all, making new shadows on the floor and dropping leaves on doorsills that had till then been bare. Cobwebs, too—sticky threads ran here and there, weaving cat's cradles from wall to wall and across the arms of the chairs. And all the time the princess slept. Slept, slept, slept, with the spindle at her side, the thumb blood on its tip no longer red.

"Hey, Morton," I said from the window. "Guess what! It's raining outside," I told him, so that maybe, if he heard me, he would know. So he wouldn't be like the princess. "It's raining really hard and there's a whole bunch of cars down there on the street. There's a big traffic jam or something and everybody's honking their horns and there's this cop waving his arms around like a maniac and blowing his whistle."

And then I thought of something else about that princess.

I had never kissed Morton before, although people were always urging me to. "How about a big birthday kiss?" they would say as somebody posed us for a photograph. Or, "Aren't you going to kiss your brother good-bye?" when my class went on a week-long trip. Who would want to kiss *him*? I'd never even kissed him with an X on the bottom of a birthday card. If I gave him a birthday card at all.

Still, it had worked on the princess, and so I pushed my lips out as though I were sucking on an egg, and I slowly lowered my face over his. "That was a kiss," I told him, so he would know, and I stepped back, licking off the taste of his skin. A small, moist circle clung to his forehead, and I watched it fade.

Then I waited to see if, like the princess, he would wake up.

CHAPTER THIRTY-FIVE

So the make-believe game—the *good* make-believe game—that came true in the end was not Blondie or First Lady or movie star or rich girl.

It was Easter egg, where I played I was a bunny in a bright plaster room. But it didn't come true the way I played it.

My mother and my father and I all got to sit around a little table, like the rabbits in the game, and we each were given little colored eggs. Sort of colored eggs. There were pictures all around us, too, as there were inside the egg, and my father, like the father rabbit, reached into his pocket every evening for a coin.

But the table was in a hospital waiting room with fluorescent pipes along the ceiling, not in an egg with a porthole full of light, and the walls were hung with posters from the zoo. My father took a quarter from his pocket, not a coin with a rabbit on its face, and the little colored eggs were M&M's. Still, though, there were only three of us, and when we got up to leave at seven-thirty each night, we would walk out together, side by side, like the three rabbits in the egg—a mother, a father, and one child.

Every evening was the same. My parents and I would get to the hospital—a big hospital, not the one where my mother works—and wait downstairs in the lobby until a bell rang and visitors could see the patients. We would sit in the same places—on three pink chairs around a table that sometimes had magazines on it, sometimes not. If it did, I would turn the pages one after the other and not read anything. After a while my father would get up and walk over to the candy machine. He would study all the packages in their little windows, as though he were trying to make up his mind, but in the end he always pulled the same plunger and a bag of M&M's would drop into the tray.

Then my mother would get up and look at the zoo posters, moving slowly from one to the other and studying their scenes as though they were famous paintings and she'd never seen them before.

Morton was allowed only two visitors at a time, and at seven o'clock, when the bell rang, my parents would go up in the elevator together while I ate my M&M's one by one, green first, yellow last. I'd hold each one between two fingers, licking its hard shell and feeling the color come off on my tongue. When I got down to the chocolate, I'd float it carefully in my mouth, not moving it at all, so it would keep a long time. The yellow one would just be turning sticky and warm when my parents would come out of the elevator and it would be my turn to go upstairs.

Always when I entered his room, I'd say the same thing: "Hello? Hello, Morton?" as though he were far away and I were speaking to him on the phone. Then I'd sit in the chair beside his bed and watch him breathe. His face was the only part of his body that I could see, although his feet and knees made cones beneath the spread. An upside-down bottle dripped something through a tube, but I couldn't tell where it went. I'd sit there for about five minutes, staring at Morton, staring at the tube, staring at the labels on the bottles next to his bed. I'd pick out a word from one of them— "sterile," maybe—and make little words from its letters: list, tire, tile, else, steel, trile. I played a game— if I could make six words or more, then Morton would wake up. Trile probably wasn't a real word, but I let it count anyway.

A television set, mounted on a shelf near the ceiling, tilted its black, blank screen toward Morton's bed. I would stare at it a long time, pretending that the figures deep inside its glass were the brother and sister in a family show and not just the reflections of Morton and of me.

Then, after another five minutes—ten, maybe—I'd get up and walk to the window. Two stone birds were carved into the corners of the building across the street, and I'd watch them as though they were real. Their wings were spread wide, and their claws were pulled up against their chests. In another moment they would maybe fly away.

If you touch stone, you'll turn to stone. Wanda used to say that, and I imagined now that long ago two real birds had flown by mistake into that big stone wall and been frozen into its corners ever since. Now and then a pigeon would approach, and I would wave my hands to warn it off.

When visiting hours were over, I'd say good-bye to Morton. "Good-bye," I'd say out loud, and I'd keep my hands behind my back as though he, too, were made of stone, and by touching him I'd harden like a statue on the floor. "Good-bye. I hope you feel better," which was a dumb thing to say, because he didn't feel anything at all. Then I'd go back down in the elevator.

Once, returning to the waiting room, I saw two old people in the pink plastic chairs where my parents had been sitting before, and I stopped still. Then I saw

[267]

that they *were* my parents, looking old, looking worried and scared, and I wondered something: Were they secretly glad, I wondered, that such a terrible thing had happened to Morton, so that at last they could love him and want him to live?

CHAPTER THIRTY-SIX

"Don't stare," my mother said, and I snapped my eyes straight ahead. We were walking through the hospital corridor and I had been looking into rooms at all the people in their beds. It was Thursday, my mother's day off, and we had come, just the two of us, to see Morton.

Four more doors and we would be at his room. I closed my eyes for a moment and pretended something: When we reached his door we would find him wide awake. He'd be sitting up in bed, with his knees bent into a hill and his eyes all the way open. He'd be staring into the blank television screen high up on the wall, and the first face he'd see after his long sleep would be his own; he would think, maybe, that it belonged to someone else—someone in a show.

I pretended something else: When he woke up he wouldn't be dumb anymore. He'd be smart. The fall would have unclogged something in his head, the way kicking a broken toy makes it run again, and he'd understand all his arithmetic and spelling. He'd get promoted to eighth grade when he went back to school, or to ninth or tenth, and he'd look different, too. When the girls at Agnes Daly asked me if my brother was cute, I'd say yes he was.

"Will he be different when he wakes up?" I asked my mother.

"How different?"

"I don't know. His brain, I mean. Will it be different?"

"Damaged, you mean? No, Mary Ella. Don't worry about that. The doctor says he'll be just the same as before."

"No, I meant . . . Oh, that's good," I said. "That's good, he'll be the same."

Somebody with a stethoscope hanging out of her pocket bumped my shoulder and hurried along the corridor. Then a whole bunch of people in white clothes ran by, going somewhere. Something was happening at the end of the hall; carts rattled and uniforms swished. Somebody shouted; I couldn't tell who. Maybe somebody had died in one of those rooms. Maybe somebody had died just that minute. People did die here. Only the day before, some doctors had come out of a room very slowly and closed the door behind them, holding the knob all the time so it made no noise at all. I twisted my neck now to make sure Morton's door was open.

Someone had moved him in his bed; he was lying on his side, not on his back, but his eyes were still tight shut. If he did wake up, the two stone birds across the way would be the first faces he would see.

I walked to the window and looked out. They were really pretty ugly, those birds. Their heads jutted out on long stone necks and their beaks hung down like hooks. What were they doing there, anyway, far, far up from the street, where no one but me could see?

"What did he *do* it for?" my mother asked from somewhere in the room. She was speaking to her listener, who had followed her through the door and settled on the wall. "What *for?*"

"To get his coal car back," I answered into the window. "It was on that other roof where it fell."

I had already told her that.

I had told her a million times.

I had told my father.

I had told the policeman when he came to our apartment the morning after the accident. "He was trying to get this train car back from where it fell on the next-door roof," I had told him that day.

No policeman had ever been in our house before,

and I gasped when I saw him at the kitchen table, all that blue filling the room. Before then, I had never even spoken to a policeman. Not aloud, anyway. I spoke to them all the time, though, in my head. *See how good I am*, I would say as I passed one on the street, and I would straighten my spine and make my face look nice. *See how I'm not stealing anything or crossing on a red light or writing bad words on walls*, and I would feel his eyes on me, liking me because I was good.

"Come in, Mary Ella," my mother had said, although I already was in. She was sitting across from the policeman, and she looked small. My father was there, too, leaning against the refrigerator door. Standing while the policeman sat. "The officer wants to ask you some questions." Officer.

I looked at him again. He was too big for the table, too big for the room, and anyway, he didn't belong in our apartment at all. He belonged outside, with cars and trucks and sidewalks, not among our dishes and cups and the little glass prism throwing rainbows on the floor. Still, I smoothed my hair back when he told me to sit down, and I pressed my knees together, and my ankles, too, the way I do when I talk to Miss Rice in her office and I want her to think I'm nice.

A thick notebook lay on the table and he smoothed

a page with the flat of his hand. "Did he always play on the roof?" he asked.

"Just that once," I told him. "The second time he wasn't playing."

"Never," my mother said. "They weren't allowed up there."

The policeman leaned over and wrote something down. Which answer, I wondered, did he pick? He looked as though he was doing schoolwork, with his forehead pressed into his hand, and once he raised his eyes to the ceiling, trying to remember the spelling of a word.

"How did the object fall?" he asked.

"The object?" I thought he meant Morton.

"The toy."

"It just fell," I told him. That's the kind of answer grown-ups hate, so I went on, wanting him to like me, to like my answers. "We were playing this game," I said, "and it fell, but not the same day Morton fell. At the beginning of the summer. When he fell he was all by himself."

"Where is the object now?" and again I thought he meant Morton.

"It's still there," I finally told him.

"It was a very expensive train," my mother added, and the policeman wrote something down then, too.

"They took an expensive toy up to the roof and threw it over the side," she went on, but she wasn't speaking to him anymore. She was speaking to her listener on the clock.

"We didn't throw it, Mom. It *fell*. We were playing that the wall was the track and there was something up ahead that the coal car bumped into. A cow," I added, and the policeman wrote something else in his book. Maybe about the cow. "And then he wanted it back. To take to the farm, because he couldn't take his collections."

At that time, that's what I really thought.

"What collections?" my mother asked.

"In those bags. Those paper things that he kept, and the bottle caps. His plastic spoons."

The policeman kept writing in his notebook, even though we weren't talking to him anymore.

"Those? That's ridiculous, Mary Ella. He didn't want to take that with him. That's just junk. He understood all that. I'd already explained to him that Mrs. Floyd wouldn't have tolerated it in her house. No other mother would."

I thought she was going to tell about how any other mother would have thrown all that stuff into the trash can, and the policeman would write that down, too, but she didn't.

"It makes no sense," she said, and my father leaned on his other foot.

He hadn't said anything the whole time.

"It makes no sense," my mother said in Morton's hospital room. "Why would he take an expensive toy up to a place like that and just throw it over the wall?"

I turned around now to look at her. "Mom," I said, "it wasn't his idea to go up there and put the train on the wall. It was Polly's. And he didn't make it fall. She did."

I hadn't told her that before, because I knew what she would answer. In fact, she answered it now. "That's why he did it? Because somebody told him to? Somebody told him to take an expensive toy like that up to the roof and drop it over the edge, and he did?" And then she asked the other thing I was afraid she would ask. "What else did he do because somebody told him to? Climb over the wall and try to get it back?"

It was a long time before I said anything.

"Yes,'" I finally answered. "Yes, he did."

CHAPTER THIRTY-SEVEN

I had found that out myself only the day before, and I hadn't meant to tell it to my mother at all.

I had found it out because I'd gone back up to the roof, which was another thing I didn't want my mother to know about, and it was Polly herself who had told me.

I'd gone up there to see the coal car, to say good-bye to it or something, or hello; I'm not sure which. *I'll go there just this once,* I'd said to myself, *and never again,* although I wasn't sure of that, either.

It had rained that morning, and flat black pools lay scattered on the tar. In one I could see, for just a moment, the white-and-purple wings of a pigeon over-head; in another the edges of a cloud. I touched the cloud with my toe and made it wobble.

Everything looked as it had the very first day I'd gone up: the chimney pipes, the antennas, the drying shirts that dangled like a stretch of paper cutouts from the line. The pigeons.

But the sun was high in the sky and the chimneys made no shadows on the tar. Also, something smelled funny. Paint, maybe, or that stuff they clean the bathrooms with in school. It nipped at the corners of my eyes, and its taste slid down my throat like a cough drop. Another thing: An empty stretch of rope, brand-new, was coiled around the crosspiece of the clothesline frame. I took it down and carried it to the wall.

The coal car lay upside down in a puddle, like a tiny shipwreck, so dark it made no image in the water. I couldn't even find it right away.

"Hey," I said, swinging the rope out to it. "Hey, wake up," as though, like Morton, it had settled into some strange, deep sleep.

I swung the rope out a few times more, and then, all at once, I felt it touch. The kiss of rope on plastic traveled like electricity into my hand and I jumped back. At the same moment a voice spoke behind me— "What smells up here?"—and I whirled around. "It smells like needles in your nose."

It was Polly.

That was the first time I'd seen her since the accident. I didn't know where she'd been all that time, and no one on the block knew, either. "I think she ran away," Deirdre said, and Ezra said she was in jail.

I wasn't sure I wanted to see her at all. I liked being up there all alone, just me and the coal car. Anyway, I couldn't think of anything to say. I didn't want to talk about Morton, but I didn't want to *not* talk about him, either.

"What are you doing here?" I finally asked.

"I don't know. What are you?"

"Nothing," I said. "Looking."

"Me too," and that's all we said for a long time.

A small puddle of rain had collected in the little hollow between the coal car's wheels, and it shimmered like dew. "Look," Polly said. "You can see its underneath."

"Yeah," I answered, and that was how we finally talked about Morton.

She bunched her fingers together after that and ran them along the top of the ledge. *"Rum-rum-rum,"* she said.

"Rum-rum-rum," I said, too, making a finger-car of my own and sliding it along after hers.

Rum-rum-rum, and together the two cars ran back and forth along their single track, smoothly, not bumping into each other, not crashing into cows, not flying over the side.

"Last stop!" Polly walked her finger-car into the air and puffed it away.

[*278*]

After that we just stood there side by side, leaning over the wall as though it were the railing of a boat and the tar a stretch of sea.

A small flock of pigeons tumbled down from somewhere and arranged themselves in a crooked row, a foot or so from the coal car. "Hey, look, M. E.," Polly said, pointing down at them. "Look at those pigeons. They're going to *sing* for us. They're all lined up, like on a stage in school, and we're the mothers who came to watch. They're going to sing 'My Country, 'Tis of Thee.' " She said "Tizzathee," like kids in kindergarten. "Which one do you want to be yours, M. E.?"

"I don't know. Maybe that one, with the neck that turns green and purple."

"Mine's the gray one on the end."

"That one?" I said, looking. She had picked a pigeon that had no colors on it at all—no stripes, no bands, no green-and-purple shimmer on its neck. All it was was a plain gray bird. "How come you want *that?*"

"I like the way it walks. It's wearing this gray cloak thing that's all tight around its ankles, and it has to take these little steps." She showed me with two fingers how it walked.

It did walk that way, sort of, but still I wondered. What was so great about that? And I wondered once again about Polly. Was she dumb or crazy or what?

How come she picked the ugliest bird in the row to be her own?

"I'm magic," she said, and I wondered if I had spoken aloud.

"What?"

"I can make pigeons do whatever I want. Watch. *Dance!*" she shouted down at them, and they all bounced off the ground. "See?"

We stood there for a long time, watching the pigeons, not saying much, and then suddenly I asked something. "Polly, remember when we were playing bug race and I told you about this kid I knew who said that make-believe games came true?"

"No."

"She said someone inside you listens to bad wishes in your head and makes them happen?"

"So what about her?"

"Well, she was right, sort of. I used to play this game a lot, just for fun, and then it came true, but all wrong."

"What game? You mean bug race?"

"No, not that kind. The kind you make up. In your head."

"You played bug race in your head?"

"No!" Why didn't she ever understand anything I said? "I made something *up*. And later it came true."

"That's dumb. Nothing comes true. Things just happen, no matter what. Hey, look now, M. E. The gray pigeon is bowing. It's *bowing*. The others all forgot to do that, but mine didn't. Come on, M. E. Clap for it. *Clap*."

Things just happen, no matter what. I tightened my ears, so the words would stick inside my head and not leak out, and I touched Polly's hand for an instant so that what she had just said would stick to my skin, too, and keep.

"Clap!" she said again, but I didn't—I was still thinking about what she'd said. "What did you make up?" she asked after a while.

"Something." And then I told her. "I made up that I lived with a mother and a father all by myself. Without a sister or a brother or anything. And now that's true, sort of."

"That's dumb. How could somebody fit inside your head? And besides, if they did that for everybody, then all the wishes would get mixed up." Suddenly, for the first time ever, she seemed almost smart. "Like, suppose *I* played that I lived with you and Morton, and *you* played that you lived with me and my grandmother. How could they make both wishes come true?" and she gave me a smile she sometimes had, where her lips stretched out wide, like a string of gum, and her eyebrows disappeared beneath her hair.

I loved her then. I loved the way she looked and I

[281]

loved the way she smiled and I loved the way she thought it was dumb that make-believe games came true.

"Let's see that," she said, taking the rope from my hand.

"Don't throw it over," I warned her, "like last time."

"I didn't throw it over last time. It jumped. It was an acrobat. This one's a snake." She wriggled the rope along the wall. "It's a poisonous snake and it could bite my hand, but it won't, because I'm magic. I'm a snake charmer, and all's I have to do is stare into its eyes and it will go to sleep. Go to sleep, you," she shouted down the wall. "SLEEP!"

The row of pigeons suddenly took flight above our heads, holding their wings straight out and sweeping around, going nowhere, looking like the kids in Interpretive Dance when they're supposed to be airplanes. "Look," Polly said, raising her head to watch them. "They're going crazy. They probably smell that stuff and they can't hold their noses because their feet won't reach. What *is* that smell, anyway?"

"I don't know," I said. "Polly, do you think we can get it back, the coal car? With the rope?"

"No. Anyway, it's not a rope. It's a snake. Come on, snake, give me a kiss," and she rubbed the fuzzy end against her mouth. "Hey, look, M. E." She was leaning far, far over the wall now, and suddenly she stopped swinging the rope. "Look! *That's* what that smell is: *paint*. On that ladder there. Orange paint. I knew it smelled orange. Orange always smells like needles."

"What ladder?" I leaned far over, too. So far over, my toes lifted off the ground and my hands slid out along the wall. "I don't see a ladder." But then I did.

CHAPTER THIRTY-EIGHT

Fastened against the wall and sticky still with bright orange paint was a row of iron rungs. It was a fire escape ladder, and it led from our roof to the rooftop down below.

"Hey," Polly said. "Where did that come from?"

I didn't answer her for a long time. "It didn't come from anywhere," I finally whispered. "It was there all the time. Attached to the wall."

"It was? That ladder?"

"Polly, it wasn't orange then. That's why we didn't see it." Even the ambulance men had missed it. The roof was dark when they had arrived, and they had used a ladder made of rope.

"What color was it then? Purple?"

"*No.* It was no color. It was—I don't know. Polly," and my face felt suddenly hot. "He could have gone down that ladder!"

"They should have painted it purple. A purple ladder. My favorite color."

"Polly!" I repeated. *"He could have climbed down that ladder!"*

"Yeah," she said. "Like this. Watch." She flung her leg over the wall and lowered herself backward down the orange steps.

"POLLY! HE COULD HAVE DONE THAT, TOO!"

"Yeah. Hey, it's still wet!" and she held out a hand stained orange on the palm. "Look! It's like mud. Orange mud. Look at *this*." She pressed both hands against the tar floor to make two perfect prints. "You know what, M. E.? We can have another club. You can be the president of this one and I can be initiated. First I have to climb down here and then I have to leave a picture of my hand on the floor. Then I have to get the coal car," she added, walking over to the puddle.

"Don't touch it!" I yelled, and she turned to look up at me. "You'll get paint on it!"

"No, I won't," and she rubbed her hands, as I knew she would, on her skirt.

Our foreheads nearly touched as we both peered down at the coal car huddled like a bird in the creases of her hand.

"Look, M. E.," she said, rocking it back and forth. "Look at the yellow. It's gray. And the red cat is brown," but I didn't speak at all. I didn't even breathe, as though the smallest stirring of air would make it lift its wings and fly away. In a little while I would hold it myself, enclosing it in my own hands like a pet mouse, and I would carry it downstairs to the box in Morton's room. I would fit it into its own special cutout and I would say, "Look who's back," to all the rest of the cars. It would wait there for Morton to wake up so he could finally take it with him to the farm, instead of the bugs. Instead of his collections. For now, though, I didn't want to touch it at all.

"The wheels don't go," Polly said, rubbing them against her thumb. "Still, it will make a good going-away present."

"Yeah, well, he won't be going away now for a while."

"Who won't?"

"Morton. He has to get better first and everything."

"I don't mean Morton. I mean *me*. *I'm* going away."

At first I thought she meant—I don't know what I thought she meant. That she was going to camp, maybe. Fresh-air camp, or she was going to visit someone. "Where are you going?"

"Back home."

"Where back home? You mean to your grandma's?"

"No. *Home* home. To my mother's."

"To your mother's? That far? Where it's yesterday sometimes? That's where?" I couldn't believe her. "When are you coming back?"

"I'm not."

"But I thought she didn't have enough money. I thought she liked your sister best. I thought you were going to stay here." And be my best friend, I wanted to say.

"Yeah, well, I'm not." She looked down once more at the coal car in her hand. "Hey, you know what, M. E.? I could fix this up, maybe, and then it could go places. All's I have to do is teach it to turn its wheels again. It forgot how, is all. Then when I make it better, it can go all over. It can go to Africa. Or Australia."

"Polly." I reached my hand out and held it open. "Let me have it now. It's Morton's coal car."

"No, it's not. It's mine. He said I could have it."

"Come on, Polly."

"He did."

"He did not. He can't even talk."

"No, *before* that, he said I could. Before he fell."

"When before?" I stared at her. "*Just* before? Polly, were you there when he fell? WERE YOU?"

She stared back. "No. How could I be? I was with you. Getting the bugs ready. Remember?"

"When, then? When did he say that?"

"I don't know. The day before, probably. The day before he fell. He said I could have it if I wanted it."

"He did not, Polly. He wanted it for himself. So he could take it with him to the farm. Instead of his collections. That's why he tried to get it."

"Oh, M. E. That's not why."

"Then why? Why did he? WHY?"

"Because I told him to."

A cloud covered the sun just then, and everything turned gray: Polly's face, her hands, the row of drying shirts, everything that should have been white. "Polly," I said, and my voice came out in a whisper. "All that afternoon, when we were waiting for him to come home from school, and then when we walked through the streets looking for him—at the movies and everywhere—did you know all along that he had gone to the roof to get the coal car? *Did* you?"

"Yeah," she said. "I didn't know he fell, though. I thought he was waiting somewhere. To surprise me."

CHAPTER THIRTY-NINE

"Polly told him to climb down that wall?" My mother stared at me. "And he did? Because she told him to?" She looked away from me now and said what I was waiting for her to say: "He would," she said to her listener on the wall. "He *would*."

For a while there was a great silence, and then suddenly the whole room was filled with the sound of a voice. Mine. "That's not true!" I yelled. "That's not true what you said—that he would. *I* would, too." I moved forward and my words shot out into her face across Morton's bed. "It could be *me* lying here, not him. It could be ME!" I had never yelled like that at my mother before, and I felt dizzy, a little. The words came out of my mouth by themselves, as though I were throwing up, and my head began to shake. "You know what I did once? I climbed up on the awning, on that awning in front of our house, and I almost fell. The only reason I didn't was it was some kind of accident.

I could have broken my neck. Justine's mother said so. Ask her. Ask anybody. My name is up there, even. I wrote my name up on the wall in chalk. And you know why? Because Polly told me to. She played a trick on me." My eyes were closed tight now, and my words came from some dark tunnel. "IT COULD BE ME! IT COULD BE ME! NOT *HIM. ME!*"

Somebody had grabbed hold of my wrists and I opened my eyes. It was my mother, standing close to me, making me stand still, making me shut up. "Be quiet," she whispered in a voice I had never heard from her before, and I was afraid of what she might do next. Kill me or something. "Be *quiet*, Mary Ella. Stop that yelling. *Stop* it! The nurses will hear you."

"Let them!" I yelled back. "Let them hear me!" My throat ached and something far inside my ears stung as each word struck. "*All* of them!"

"Mary *Ella!*" My mother's voice was getting loud too. "Be *still.* Don't yell like that. They'll think . . ." but she fell silent: She didn't know how to finish. "They'll think . . ." and she stopped again. What *would* they think, anyway, all those nurses listening to me make all that noise while they glided so softly along the hall?

"They'll think there's a *cow* in here!" my mother yelled.

"Cows don't yell in hospitals!" I yelled back, and

then my voice dropped and so did hers. We just looked at each other and the next thing I knew she was laughing. *Really* laughing. The way Polly and I had laughed when we made faces on our noses in the mirror that day. With tears. They washed over her cheeks and got her hair all wet and her ears too.

I'd never seen her laugh like that before. I'd never seen her laugh much at all, in fact, and I wanted the moment to last. "Cows don't yell in hospitals," I said again, although I wasn't sure she was laughing at that. I wasn't sure what she was laughing at, really, but suddenly I began to laugh with her. Tears burst from my eyes too—laugh tears—and then, because we didn't want to look at each other with our faces all wet like that and twisted up, we hid ourselves on each other's shoulders. For a long time we stood there, together, shaking and sniffing, holding on—hugging, sort of— while our faces grew wetter and wetter.

"Visiting hours are over." Someone in a pink uniform pushed a mop into the room. "Hi, Big Boy," she said to Morton. "How's it going?" and she pushed the mop out into the hall again. She hadn't looked at my mother and me at all.

After a while we both quieted down, but we still held on to each other, not moving. "Mom," I whispered when my voice came back. "Don't be mad at Morton. Be mad at me, too."

"I'm not mad at either of you," she whispered back. "I love you both."

We didn't move after that, and her head lay on my shoulder for a long time.

"Time to go!" somebody called through the door, but we stayed where we were, holding each other for a long, long time.

"They said we have to go," I said finally, and I slipped out from her arms. I took a tissue from the box next to Morton's bed and wiped my tears. I'd dried my eyes too, when Polly and I had laughed together, but that time the tissue had turned purple and I'd saved it for always in my drawer. It lies there even now; I see it every day when I go to get my socks.

My mother wiped her face and nose, too, but not on a tissue. On the back of her hand, like Morton. "Mom," I said. "We should go," but she just went over to Morton's bed and leaned over him. Then, making scissors out of two fingers, she grasped a piece of his hair and slid it back and forth as though it were a strip of satin or of seaweed; as though it were smooth and slippery and she liked the way it felt. Suddenly she began to speak to him. Tiny sounds came from her lips, and she tilted his head to one side so he could receive them into his ear. They fell, one by one, like pennies dropping into a jar. "Morton," I heard her say, "listen to me. *Listen*," and I turned back to the window, because the words were just for him.

A bird—a real one—flew over to the stone head across the way and settled on the beak. *Look out*, I whispered in my head, *you'll turn to stone*, but it didn't. It shifted about from foot to foot for a while, as though it were dancing on hot sand, and then it lifted itself into the sky. I followed it until it was just a speck.

My mother continued to murmur behind me, pretending that Morton could hear her, just as she used to pretend, when she spoke to her listener, that he could not. Suddenly, her voice grew loud, making me jump. "Listen to me, Morton! *Listen!* You're going to get better, do you hear me? Do you? You're going to get better and you're going to come back home. We're all waiting for you there."

He wasn't going to the farm after all. He was going to come home. He wasn't a bad influence on me; I wasn't a bad influence on him. We were going to be a family, like the one in the egg, except the child rabbit now would have a brother.

If he woke up.

SEPTEMBER

CHAPTER FORTY

They took the awning down today. It was up when I
left for school in the morning, down when I came
home. Sky was stretched across its frame now, instead
of canvas, and I stood with my head back for a while,
looking between the long skinny bars.

Summer is over.

Not only that. Today was the first day of school.
Agnes Daly always opens on this day—the last
Wednesday of September, weeks after everybody else
has gone back.

All the kids were standing around talking when I
walked into my new classroom, but they fell silent as
soon as they saw me, so I knew right away that they
had all heard about Morton.

I was hoping they hadn't. I was hoping they didn't
even know I had a brother at all. Mostly, I was hoping
they hadn't heard how the accident had happened.
Falling from a roof was a poor kids' thing to do, not

a rich kids', and I didn't want them to think I was poor. Rich kids didn't fall from roofs. Rich kids didn't go up on roofs in the first place. Rich kids played where there was lots of grass and trees, like at camp. Rich kids were *watched*.

I didn't look at anybody as I went to my new desk and sat down. One of the wonderful things about being a lower or upper senior at Agnes Daly is that you get a real desk, like the kind teachers use, with big drawers on the sides for your papers and a nice blue blotter on top. Our names were printed on folded strips of cardboard, as though we were the president of a company or something. Iris's name was on the desk next to mine, and I tried to see whose name was on the one next to hers. Rhoda's, probably.

I ran my hand across the new blue blotter, smoothing it, and then I opened each drawer, pretending to look for something. I put my pen in one and my notepad in another. After that I sat very still, with my eyes on the front wall, as I do at a play when the curtain is about to go up. Soon the new teacher would come in and everyone would be quiet. Quiet because of *her*, and not because of me.

Later, though, when I thought everyone had forgotten I was there, Iris sent me a note. It bounced across my blotter like a lame bird and fell into my lap. "I heard about your brother," it read. "Love, Iris." I stared at it a long time, wondering whether she was being mean or not. "Love," it said. "Love, Iris." Why would anyone who was being mean write "Love"? Unless it was some kind of trick. Something she and Rhoda had thought up together, but when I looked around I discovered that Rhoda wasn't at any of the desks. Maybe she didn't go to Agnes Daly anymore. Maybe Iris was looking for a new friend. I read her note again and looked up at her. She gave me a smile.

"I heard about your brother." What, I wondered, had she heard? That he had fallen on his head while trying to get a toy from the next-door roof because some girl had told him to, and that he had lain unconscious in a hospital bed for days?

Or that one day, three weeks ago, while he lay there, a strange thing had happened that no one at the hospital could explain?

It was the day before Polly left for good, and I was walking down the hospital hall, holding a box in my hand and rehearsing in my head what I would say to Morton when I sat beside him in his room.

I had started visiting him in the afternoons then, by myself, going there on the bus and coming back before my mother got home from work. There was nothing to do at home by then; everyone else had gone back to school and I didn't feel like seeing Polly anymore. Besides, I liked to talk to Morton, even though he couldn't hear me. *Because* he couldn't hear me.

"Guess what," I was going to say to him this time. "Your coal car isn't on that roof anymore. Polly got it back. Morton, there was a ladder up there that went from our roof to the one next door. It was there all the *time*, only we didn't know about it, and Polly climbed down and got your coal car back."

Somebody was wheeling a bundle of something on a long cart, and I stepped aside to let it go by. After it passed, I realized the bundle was a person, stretched out straight and still under a sheet.

"But Morton, this is the bad part: She's keeping it for herself. She says she needs it for something. She says she has to have it, even when I told her it was yours and everything. Even when I told her it cost a whole lot of money." In fact, that was all I had told her that afternoon. That and, "Polly, you can't do that," but of course she could. She'd already done it.

Another cart hurried by, making a little breeze, and I held the box close to my body so it wouldn't blow away. "She says it's magic," I was going to tell him, and I felt myself begin to cry, as I had up on the roof that day when Polly snapped her fingers over the coal car and ran with it down the stairs. "She says it has special powers. I don't know what she says. Morton, she really isn't my friend anymore, and anyway, she's going away. She's going back to live with her mother, where it's yesterday sometimes, and we won't see the coal car again, or her, either."

Then I was going to tell him about the present I had brought him. "But I brought you something else instead, Morton," I was going to say, and I would open the box right in front of his face. "Look," I'd say, even though his eyes would still be closed. "This is for you."

I held the box up to my ear then and gave it a small shake, liking the click I heard against the cardboard. It would be a good surprise, and I wondered if somehow in his deep, deep sleep, Morton would know that I was there and had brought him something nice.

More carts rolled by and people were running along the hall. Something was going on down there—something bad, probably—and all of a sudden I saw that, for the first time ever, the door to Morton's room was tightly shut.

I stood still as a stone.

Up until that moment I had thought that nothing worse could happen to Morton than what had already happened. He would go on forever, I thought, asleep in his bed, like the princess. Or he would wake up.

I closed my eyes. *Don't let anything happen to him*, I whispered. *Don't let it, don't let it, don't let it.* And then I walked up to his room and faced the door.

Everything was silent on the other side, and I stood

there a long time, listening, not hearing anything, staring at the number—435—on the polished wood. Four three five, I read to myself, as though it were a message left especially for me. Four hundreds, three tens, five ones. Four red sticks, three blue sticks, five green sticks. Say that, Morton. Say it after me. *Say it!*

Suddenly, on the other side of the door I heard something. *Scratching*, it was, and I called out, "Who's there?" thinking—I don't know what I was thinking. That Morton was trying to get out, maybe, or someone else had already moved in. "Who's *there?*" and all at once the door swung open and I stood face-to-face with Polly.

She was wearing her grandmother's skirt and blouse again, and in her hand she held a piece of chalk.

"What are you doing here?" I finally asked. I had meant to whisper, but a half shout had come out instead. "What happened to Morton?"

"Nothing." I didn't know which question she was answering, but by then I saw that Morton was still lying in his bed, breathing in and out, the same as always, with his eyes tight shut. A paper bag, squashed flat like a sweet potato, lay at his feet. Who put that there? I wondered, but I didn't ask. I didn't say anything. I turned my back to Polly and closed the door.

"Hey," I said suddenly, staring at the door. "You're

not supposed to do that! You're not supposed to write your name on things in a hospital! You can get germs all over the place that way. Look what you *did*! You put chalk germs all over his door." I began to rub the P with my fist.

"What's in the box?" she asked, but I didn't answer. I didn't even turn around.

"I said, what's in the box?"

"Nothing." The chalk wasn't coming off, and I wet it with a finger.

"Hey, Morton," she said, and I could see from the edge of my eye that she was moving over to his bed. "Morton, you know what? You look like a fish, with your mouth open like that. Doesn't he, M. E.? Look at him. He's just like a fish."

What kind of chalk was that, anyway? It didn't even *smear*.

"Hey, you know what, Morton? I brought you something. Guess what it is." She was reaching now for the bag at his feet. "Here, open it," but she was holding it out to me, not to him, and in another moment she was standing at my side. "Take it, Mary Ella," she said. She had opened up the bag and was putting something cold in my hand.

For a moment I didn't even recognize it. It had been painted shiny orange, and a brand-new cat—a circle with whiskers, a circle with spots, and a long, looped tail—had been drawn in Magic Marker on each side. The wheels were polished clean and they spun when I pushed them with my thumb.

"Go ahead, M. E.," Polly said. "Give it to him," and in a moment I was walking across the room to his side.

"Morton," I said. I reached under the covers for his hand. "Hey, Morton. This is for you." I spoke the words I had rehearsed in the hall, to go with the present I had brought. "Look." Then, carefully, carefully, as though the lines across his palm were a stretch of silver track, I settled each wheel in place.

"Hey, Morton, you know what?" I said. "We can go somewhere in this now. All of us. We can all go to Africa. You and me and Polly. Or Australia. We can make ourselves really small, and we can shrink all our stuff, too, and take it along. You can be the conductor, Morton, and collect all the tickets. Oh, and guess what else," I added, remembering. "I brought two other passengers."

"Oh, hey!" Polly cried out as I emptied the little box into my hand. "The bugs! Where'd *they* come from?"

"They were in the bathroom," I told her. "Next to the tub, except I don't know how they got there." How *had* they gotten there, anyway? The last I knew they were in the boxcar. "Maybe they pushed the door open," I began to say, "with their . . ." but then I stopped. Something had suddenly changed in the room, and Polly and I both leaned forward from either side of Morton's bed, to stare down into Morton's face.

"Look, M. E.!" Polly whispered.

One day last spring, right out in the yard at Agnes Daly, a baby bird tumbled from its nest and landed on a patch of dirt beneath a tree. Joseph was the one who saw it first. "Hey, look!" he called out. "A broken bird! Let's fix it up and keep it for a pet." But by the time we all collected around it, it had stopped moving, and Joseph said, "Never mind. It's dead."

It wasn't, though. Someone touched its body with a stick, and all at once its wings began to stir. Slowly, very slowly, they began to lift from its body, to *peel*, really, like skin from an apple, and to stretch farther and farther into the air, until at last they pointed to the sky and carried the bird off the ground.

And that was the way Morton's eyelids moved when suddenly they lifted from his eyes that afternoon: They *peeled* open, like the skin from an apple, like the wings of that bird. Polly's head and mine nearly touched as we bent across his bed, watching, and we matched our breathing to each other's, to make less noise. Tiny breaths they were, coming both together, and once, when Morton's eyelids stiffened and we thought they'd shut again, we even gasped together, in a single small sound like a half-swallowed cry.

And then, all at once, his lids were up, all the way up, with his lashes reaching almost to his brows. His eyeballs wobbled slightly, like marbles coming to rest, but finally they locked into place, and the first thing Morton saw after his long, long sleep was not his image in the screen or the pair of stone birds on the wall across the way.

It was Polly and me.

I can't remember how long it took, but suddenly the room was filled with people—people in white, people in green, people in pink. Someone had a thin paper mask across her mouth, and it puffed like a balloon at every word she spoke.

"It's the strangest thing," she said.

"It's a miracle."

"All they did was put that thing in his hand."

"It's magic."

Morton was propped halfway up on his pillows by then and his eyes were still wide open. He held the little coal car in his hand and slowly, very, very slowly, he moved it across the white spread, leaving thin trails. His lips moved a little, as though he were kissing the air or sipping at a straw.

"He's saying something," someone said. A nurse.

"What's he saying?"

"Nothing, just sounds. That happens sometimes."

I looked across to Polly and she looked back at me. Together, with Morton, we whispered to each other. *"Rum-rum-rum."*

CHAPTER FORTY-ONE

I didn't know what to write back to Iris. The only answer I can ever think of when someone says something nice to me is "Same to you." "Same to you," I reply when people say "Have a nice summer" on the last day of school, and "Same to you" when they say "Good luck on your midterm." Once I even said that when someone wished me happy birthday.

But I couldn't say "Same to you" to someone who told me she'd heard about my brother. Even if she meant to be nice. Besides, I still wasn't sure that she *was* being nice. So all I wrote back was "He's better now." I signed it M. E., and I left out the "Love."

"That's good, Mary Ella, that he's better," she said to me at yard time. We had both been tagged out of dodgeball, and we were sitting on a ledge, waiting for the game to be over. "I didn't even know you had a brother until my mother said."

"No. Well, I do."

"How old is he?"

"Fourteen."

"Fourteen? Is he cute?"

"No. He's funny-looking."

"Is he nice, though?"

"Sort of. Yeah. He does things that are nice sometimes."

"Like what?"

"I don't know. He thinks up nice things to play."

"What grade is he in?"

I paused for just a moment. "Seventh."

"*Seventh?* He's fourteen and that's all he's in? The same as you? How come?"

"I don't know. It takes him a long time to learn things."

Other kids were getting tagged out, too, and they lined up next to us on the ledge.

"Who?" Peggy asked. "Who takes a long time to learn things?"

"My brother."

"You mean because he fell and everything?"

"No. He was always like that."

We sat there for a while and then Iris said, "I'm starting a club, Mary Ella. You want to be in it? It's a makeup club. We meet in the bathroom and we put on lipstick. You want to join?"

*   *   *

I put my new books down in a careful pile under the awning and swung on the V-shaped legs at the curb. If I leaned way back I could see, or I *thought* I could see, a few pale flecks where I'd chalked my name on the brick. THIS IS M. E.'S AWNING, it had said up there once. That was the first time I'd ever written on a wall, and I remembered how the chalk crumbled on the bumps, making pale-blue dust that fell like tiny snow. That was the first time I'd ever written on *anything* where you weren't supposed to write, and I thought then that it would be the last.

But as it happened, it wasn't.

Just before Polly and I left Morton's room, that afternoon when he first opened up his eyes and all those people in their white and pink and green hospital suits crowded around his bed, I took the piece of chalk from Polly's hand and I wrote something underneath her name on the door.

LOVES M. E. AND MORTON is what I wrote, and I enclosed it in a long, uneven heart.

A row of pigeons had settled on an antenna on the roof, and I stared at them, upside down, from the awning bars, just as I had stared at Polly back in June when she first walked down the street. From where I watched, they all looked alike—gray and plain, like the one Polly had picked to be her own, with stiff dark cloaks that narrowed at their feet.

I stared at them so long that when I closed my eyes they sprang up inside my lids, pale pink now and flat as paper—five birds pasted on a green paper sky. I held them there until they faded away, and I thought about Polly and her favorite pigeon and about how she liked it best because it had a funny walk. And then, suddenly, I understood what Polly was all about.

She wasn't dumb and she wasn't crazy.

She was magic, just as she had always said.

Not the kind of magic that can shrink things or make bugs win a race. Not the wand kind, or the trick kind either. Not that. The *other* kind; the kind of magic that can make things wonderful. She made the pigeon wonderful. She made Morton wonderful. Maybe she made me wonderful, too.

I slid my heels out into the street and brought my shoulders down low so I could see the pigeons even better, and then, all at once, for the first time ever and without even trying, I turned a somersault. Just like that! One minute I was leaning back to see a row of birds, and the next I had twirled over, with my feet behind me and my arms stretched backward on the bars in a sudden, perfect flip, quick and neat and wonderful. I had been wrong about how you're supposed

[311]

to lean your head way back and look at the sidewalk. The trick is, you have to look up at the roof.

I heard voices coming from the corner after that; the public-school kids were on their way home, but I didn't turn my head. I wanted them to see my somersault, but I didn't want them to *know* I wanted them to see it. So I just flipped over, back and forth, looking like Ezra and Charles when they stand around sometimes and swing key chains. As if I didn't care.

"Hey, look," I heard someone say. "Look at Mary Ella! Look what she can do!" It was Morton, and I straightened up so I could see him.

Today was *his* first day back at school, too, three weeks late. I looked down the block, but I couldn't find him right away. He was walking behind some other kids, but not *way* behind, and his clothes were like everybody else's. He was wearing the new jeans my mother had bought him and a new shirt with a football number on it. She had bought both of us new clothes for school—nice clothes. We got to pick out what we wanted, and his were as nice as mine. Also, he was talking to someone, but I didn't see who.

"Hey, Mary Ella," he said when he reached our front door. "That's nice, the way you do that," and I turned one more somersault—quick and neat and perfect—just for him. So he could watch me and like what I could do.

[312]